I0620321

THE
CABIN

A murder mystery

W.D. FROLICK

Author: W.D. FROLICK

WDF Publishing

www.wdfpublishing.com

ISBN 978-0-9950554-0-7

e-book ISBN 978-0-9950554-1-4

© Copyright 2016 by W. D. Frolick. All rights reserved.
First Revised Edition August 2019
Second Revised Edition March 2023

No part of this book may be reproduced in any form or by any electronic
or mechanical means, including information storage and retrieval systems,
without written permission from the publisher, except by a reviewer
who may quote brief passages in a review. This book is a work of fiction.
Names, characters, incidents, and events are products of the author's
imagination. Any resemblance to actual events, locales, organizations, or
persons, living or dead, is purely coincidental.

ACKNOWLEDGEMENTS

I want to thank Chief Josh Ewing of the Orono, Maine, Police Department for taking time from his busy schedule to answer my questions.

To Administrative Assistant Jessica Mason of the Orono Police Department, thank you for your time and the courtesy you extended to me on the telephone. I also wish to thank you for the informative tour of the police department during my research visit to your area.

I wish to thank Rose for challenging me to write this novel. Your support, love, and encouragement helped me through all the ups and downs during the writing process.

Even though I decided to remove the hospital scene from the novel, I would like to thank Shari A., Patient Relations Department at Eastern Maine Medical Center in Bangor, for her help with understanding the layout and workings of that beautiful facility.

Christine Foster, thank you for your help regarding the rivers and lakes in the Orono area. Rose and I enjoyed our conversation with you during lunch at the Penobscot Golf & Country Club.

CHAPTER 1

NYPD homicide detective Buckley John Woods, known as Buck Woods, sat staring out the window of the Starbucks on East 161st Street in the Bronx.

Ominous black clouds now hid the brilliant mid-morning sun that had shone through the window just a few minutes earlier. It was early December, and New York City streets were still bone dry.

The forecast called for a large dumping of snow by the end of the afternoon, just in time for rush hour. Buck dreaded the thought of winter. He envied his father, now retired and living in Florida. Turning away from the window, he saw his partner, Detective Cheryl Jenkins, approach. She carried a tray containing a couple of powdered doughnuts and two cups of steaming black coffee. Cheryl sat down opposite Buck and placed the tray in front of him.

"Thanks, partner," he said. "It looks like we're in for a doozy of a storm. It would be nice to get a little snow for Christmas, but from the look of those clouds, we might get more than we bargained for."

Cheryl Jenkins, an attractive woman in her early forties, had been Buck's partner for three years. She had intelligent brown eyes, shoulder-length black hair, full red lips, a bright, captivating smile, and radiated a glow of self-confidence. She was married to a New York City firefighter, and Cheryl and John Jenkins were the proud parents of two beautiful young girls, Jessie, eight, and Carolyn, ten.

She laughed. "I'm sure the girls would like snow for Santa's sleigh. I'd say that won't be a problem looking at those clouds. Trying to get home tonight could be a nightmare."

"Thank God, I don't have to worry about that," Buck said. "My condo's not far from the precinct, so I can walk home or take the bus. If it's a quiet day, you should take off early and avoid all the mess and confusion."

"That would be great," Cheryl sighed. "My drive usually takes about forty-five minutes at the best of times. If I have to drive through a snowstorm, it could take two to three hours, maybe longer. It depends on how fast the plows can clear the roads."

"Do you have any plans for Christmas?" Buck asked.

"I've booked the week off between Christmas and the New Year. I intend to enjoy some quality time with my family. We'll take the girls skating, to a movie, and relax. I've invited my mom and dad over for Christmas dinner. For New Year's evening, John and I plan to stay home and watch the celebration from Times Square."

"Sounds good," Buck said. "After the crazy year we've had, you deserve some downtime with your family. Hopefully, all the nut jobs will also take a vacation, and we won't have to deal with homicides."

"That would be great, but I wouldn't count on it. What about you, Buck? Do you have any plans for Christmas?"

Just as Buck was about to reply, two muffled gunshots rang out. A tall, slim man dressed in a Santa Claus suit darted from the mom-and-pop convenience store across the street. He held a pistol in his right hand and clutched a plastic bag in his left hand.

"Holy shit," Buck said, almost choking on his coffee. "I think Santa just robbed the convenience store."

Without a word, Cheryl sprang into action, and In her hast, she knocked over her cup spilling coffee in all directions.

"Wait up," Buck yelled as Cheryl headed out the door.

On his way, he stopped and went inside the convenience store. He found a dead Asian woman on the floor behind the counter, lying face up with two bullet holes in her chest, surrounded by blood. Buck glanced around but didn't see anyone else in the store. The cash register drawer was wide open, and all the bills were missing.

Buck pulled out his cell phone and called dispatch with the details. Spotting a police officer walking the beat, Buck went outside, waved him over, and flashed his badge.

"The store clerk has just been robbed and murdered. Secure

the area, and don't let anyone in the store," Buck said. "I've called dispatch, and a CSU team should be here soon."

"Will do," the young officer said.

Buck took off in the direction Cheryl had gone. He spotted her running like a gazelle a few blocks up the street, hot on the killer's heels. Cheryl ran five miles every day and was in excellent condition.

Buck worked out at the gym and ran regularly but was not a speedy runner. He ran as fast as he could but did not gain ground. Cheryl increased the distance between them with each passing second.

Up ahead, the killer turned into an alley and disappeared. Several seconds later, Buck heard two rapid gunshots. When he arrived, Cheryl lay motionless on the pavement, and Santa had disappeared.

Buck knelt by her side. Cheryl was still alive. She had a bullet wound in her chest and another on her right shoulder. As blood spurted from her chest wound, he pulled out his handkerchief and pressed it firmly over the hole but did little to stem the bleeding. Cheryl was losing blood rapidly. He fished out his phone and dialed.

"911. What is your emergency?"

"Police officer down. Send an ambulance immediately." He gave their location and pleaded, "Please hurry!"

Buck cradled Cheryl in his arms and whispered, "Hang on, Cheryl, hang on. You're going to make it. Just stay with me. Hold on."

With eyes half-opened and glazed, she managed a weak smile and softly whispered, "He hid behind the dumpster—ambushed me. Tell John and the girls I love them."

"You can tell them yourself, partner. You're going to get through this. Help is on the way. Stay with me." She began to choke up blood. Her smile faded, and her eyes closed. "Cheryl, Cheryl," Buck cried, but she didn't hear him. He felt her neck for a pulse—nothing.

"Shit, shit, shit!" Buck barked, staring up at the black sky.

Snow had started falling, and the cold wind sent a shiver down his spine. In the distance, a siren wailed. Buck stood up just in time to see the killer dash from behind a parked car to a fire escape ladder, and he pulled it down and began climbing as fast as he could.

Buck dashed to a spot below the ladder and yelled, "Police! Stop, or I'll shoot."

Santa turned and aimed his pistol. Quickly, Buck moved to his right and ducked just as the bullet narrowly missed his head. Before the killer could shoot again, Buck fired two shots. Like a diver on a high board in the Olympics, the killer did a backward flip and landed with a bone-crunching splat on the pavement, dead before he hit the ground.

Buck stood over the body and, in a rage, shouted, "You fucking bastard! I hope you burn in hell!"

Just as Buck arrived back at Cheryl's body, an ambulance came screeching to a stop, and a middle-aged man and a younger woman paramedic jumped out and rushed over to Cheryl.

Buck showed his badge and began to speak rapidly. "I'm Detective Woods, and the victim is my partner Detective Cheryl Jenkins. The perp we were chasing hid behind," Buck pointed, "that dumpster over there, and he jumped out and ambushed her. She didn't stand a chance. By the time I got here, she was barely alive. A few seconds later, Cheryl died in my arms. If I hadn't stopped at the convenience store, I would've gotten here sooner, and maybe I could've saved her."

"So sorry, Detective," the female paramedic said sympathetically.

"We got here as fast as we could," the male paramedic said.

Buck took out his cell phone and called dispatch. He informed the desk sergeant about Cheryl's death and his killing of the suspect. He gave his location and asked, "Has a CSU team been sent to the convenience store?"

"Yes," the sergeant replied. "Sit tight, and I'll send a squad car with a couple of officers to secure the area and another CSU team. I'll inform Captain Robertson about the situation."

A few minutes passed, and Buck's phone rang. It was his boss, Captain Shelia Robertson.

"Hello, Captain," Buck said, his voice strained.

"Buck, I've just heard the horrible news about Cheryl. I don't want you working the crime scene, and I'm sending two detectives to relieve you. A couple of IAB people are on their way to take your statement. I want to see you in my office when you're available."

"Okay, Captain."

Captain Shelia Robertson, a career police officer, had worked her way through the ranks to her current position. An African-American in her mid-fifties, she had a serious but pleasant personality. Her short, curly hair had primarily turned gray from the stress of her job. She was a little on the plump side due to several years behind a desk with very little time to exercise. Her wire-framed glasses gave her a grandmotherly look, and she always wore pearl earrings. Captain Robertson was a fair and competent administrator, equally respected by her subordinates and superiors.

Thirty minutes later, the CSU team arrived. Buck stood in a daze, watching as they exited the van. He intercepted the ME, Dr. Hector Rodriguez, a short, stout, balding forensic pathologist in his early fifties, was heading straight toward Cheryl's body. Buck had worked many homicides with Dr. Rodriguez over the last several years. They were on a first-name basis and shared a mutual respect for one another.

As he approached, Dr. Rodriguez, seeing it was Buck, stopped. "Buck, what do we have here?

"Hello, Hector. I guess you don't know. It's my partner, Cheryl Jenkins. She was chasing a murder suspect, and he ambushed her. I arrived too late, and she died a few seconds later. The perp tried to kill me, but luckily, he missed me, and I shot him in self-defense. His body is over there," Buck pointed, "under that fire escape ladder."

"So sorry, Buck. I've only known Detective Jenkins for a few years. It's a real shame—such a tragedy, my friend. From what I hear, Cheryl was an excellent cop."

"Yes, Hector, Cheryl was a terrific cop! It's a real tragedy. It all happened so damn fast, and I'm still trying to understand it all."

Fifteen minutes later, Buck filled in Cameron and Wentworth, the two detectives Captain Robertson had sent to relieve him.

When two Internal Affairs Bureau (IAB) detectives arrived, he explained what had happened.

Buck's head was still at the crime scene as he sat in Captain Robertson's office. He couldn't get the image of Cheryl lying dead on the pavement out of his mind.

"Thanks for coming in, Buck," Captain Robertson said. "I'm so sorry to hear about Cheryl. She was one hell of a cop, and we'll all miss her dearly. If you're up to it, I'd like to hear what transpired this morning." When Buck failed to answer, she asked, "Buck, are you okay?"

Buck was staring at the floor. "I don't know if I'll ever be okay," he said, lifting his head and looking directly into Captain Robertson's eyes. "It all happened so fast that it seems like a bad dream—more like a nightmare."

Buck took a minute to gather his thoughts and slowly outline the chain of events, starting at the coffee shop. Captain Robertson listened without interruption, and when he finished, a little emotional, she said, "Thanks for telling me what happened. I know it wasn't easy talking about it so soon. If it's any consolation, I lost a partner many years ago as a homicide detective. It still haunts me. You want to blame yourself and think they would still be here today if I had done something differently. I found out you can't keep second-guessing yourself. If you do, it will drive you crazy, and you'll never be able to function properly as a cop again. I suggest you take time off. Go on vacation or take a sabbatical. It would help if you had time to heal. Take it one day at a time and try to forget what happened today. It wasn't your fault! Remember that. It might help if you chat with Dr. Dale Saunders, our in-house psychologist."

Buck ignored her suggestion to speak with the shrink and said, "It pains me to think about her family. Cheryl's two little girls and her husband will be devastated. Having this happen any time of the year is bad enough, but this close to Christmas is even worse. I don't know what I'm going to say to them. I would have gladly given my own life for hers. Sometimes life is so damn unfair."

"Yes, Buck, I agree. Life tests us every day, especially in this job.

Sometimes it's hard to pick up the pieces and carry on. Sticking your head in the sand like an ostrich won't change things or bring back the people you love and care about. Sometimes God puts up roadblocks and obstacles and works in mysterious ways. We need to have faith. Please don't worry about informing Detective Jenkins' family. That's my job, and I'll take care of it."

"Thanks, Captain. I don't think I can face Cheryl's family just yet. I hate to say this, but I've lost faith in God."

"I'm sorry you feel that way, Buck. Give yourself a few days to process what happened today. Speaking with Dr. Saunders can't hurt, and she might be able to help. Would you like me to set up a meeting?"

"Why don't I sleep on it for a few days."

"Okay, Buck, as you wish. Go home. Take a few days off, and we can talk again soon."

Without saying another word, Buck stood up and left the building.

His head was still spinning. Instead of going home, he went to the nearest bar and got shitfaced drunk. The bartender cut him off just after four o'clock and called Buck a taxi. When he arrived at his condo, after several tries, he managed to fit his key into the lock. He staggered into his bedroom and, flopping, fully clothed, onto the bed, passed out instantly.

Buck spent a few days in his condo, drinking and puking his guts out. He had barely eaten a thing, and his head felt the size of a watermelon. Finally, on the third day, Buck decided it was time to face what had happened to his partner. Remembering Captain Robertson's suggestion, he picked up the phone and made an appointment to see the in-house shrink, Dr. Saunders.

St. Raymond Catholic Church was jam-packed five days after the shooting, overflowing with mourners. Police officers representing cities and towns across the United States attended Cheryl's funeral.

Captain Robertson gave a touching and emotional eulogy. She talked about Cheryl's bravery and commitment to her family, community, and NYPD.

The interment occurred at St. Raymond Cemetery on Lafayette

Avenue in the Bronx. A biting north wind chilled the crowd standing on the snow-covered ground at the graveside. Buck felt his heart was about to break as he watched Cheryl's two little girls, Jessie and Carolyn. They held hands with their father, tears streaming down their cheeks, and slowly walked up to the flag-draped coffin with a single red rose. As they placed the roses on Cheryl's casket, Buck gulped hard, feeling a lump in his throat. As tears filled his eyes, he turned away, fumbling for his handkerchief.

After the priest had said final prayers and blessed the casket, Buck composed himself and worked up the courage to approach Cheryl's husband, John, and his daughters.

"John, I'm so sorry for your loss," Buck whispered, his voice cracking. Wrapping his arms around him, he gave John a gentle hug. "I feel so guilty, and maybe I could've saved her if I had gotten to Cheryl sooner."

"Thanks, Buck," John replied. "Please don't blame yourself. Captain Robertson said that you did everything possible, and it wasn't your fault. I'm glad you're safe, and I thank God you got Cheryl's killer. In my job as a firefighter and your job, we put our lives on the line every day. I've lost friends in the fire department—several on 9/11, alone. It's tough, but we can't blame ourselves. We have to suck it up and carry on. We've still got a job to do."

"John, if there's anything I can do, please let me know. Again, I'm so sorry."

"Thanks, Buck, I appreciate it."

Buck knelt and looked into the tear-filled eyes of Jessie and Carolyn. He kissed them each on the cheek, fighting to hold back tears, and said, "Your mom told me to tell you and your dad how much she loved you. Although you can't see her, your mother is watching you from heaven. She will always be with you—always!"

As his eyes moistened, Buck stood up, softly said goodbye, turned, and slowly walked away. Facing John Jenkins and his daughters was the hardest thing he had experienced since a tragic event when he was a teenager.

A few days later, after a thorough investigation, the IAB report stated that Buck had acted in self-defense in the shooting of Cheryl's killer and was cleared of any wrongdoing.

Cheryl's killer, twenty-eight-year-old Harvey Hubert, had a long rap sheet. Recently released from prison after serving several years for armed robbery, he had been in trouble with the law since his teenage years.

After several sessions with Dr. Dale Saunders, Buck's guilt began to subside. Gradually he began to resemble his old self again, but he wasn't ready to return to work and mentor a new partner. Over the years, he had accumulated a few months of unused vacation time. He had a brief meeting with Captain Robertson, and together they decided it was a good idea for Buck to use his vacation time and get away for a while.

A few days before Christmas, Buck flew to Sarasota to visit his retired father. He ran every morning, golfed with his dad, relaxed on the beach, swam in the ocean, went deep-sea fishing, and read various novels, including every James Patterson and Stuart Woods book he could find. After two months, Buck began to get bored. Feeling much better, he returned to NYC and continued his life.

After a month on the job, the guilt returned. Buck's heart wasn't into solving murders and chasing bad guys. He worked out a sabbatical with the NYPD. The arrangement allowed him to return to the job or take early retirement after six months. With that settled, he decided it was time to go home to Orono, Maine, and face the demons from his past.

CHAPTER 2

Buck made arrangements to rent his furnished one-bedroom condo to a friend, a young, unmarried NYPD drug squad detective. On his way out, he stopped by the manager's office and left a set of keys for his new tenant. In the underground parking garage, he threw two suitcases into his newly purchased Chevy Silverado, slid behind the wheel, and took off. It didn't take long for the smog and high-rises of New York City to recede in his rear-view mirror.

Buck felt good! There wasn't a cloud in the sky, and the bright sun warmed him as it shone through his window. As he cruised down I-95, he sang along to the Garth Brooks song, "Friends in Low Places," blasting from the multi-speaker stereo system.

As he drove, he began to reminisce. He was dying to see his old hometown. Was it still the same? Had it changed since he was last home? He wondered if his best friend, Jim Barkowsky, was still a detective with the town police force. Was their old watering hole, Kelly's Bar & Grill, still the local hangout?

Buck's grandfather, Bill Woods, passed away several years ago and willed him his log cabin. It sat on two acres of land on Pushaw Lake, a short drive from his hometown of Orono. His grandparents were married for over fifty years, and his grandfather became a recluse after his grandmother died. Suffering from Alzheimer's disease, his grandmother passed away at seventy-nine. After her death, his grandfather began to drink heavily, wasted away, and lost his desire to live. He died two years later from what Buck suspected was a broken heart. As all these thoughts ran through his head, Buck hadn't noticed a state trooper sitting on his bumper. Suddenly, he was jarred back to reality when a siren shrieked, and he saw flashing lights in his rear-view mirror.

Buck checked his speedometer, and he wasn't speeding. Why am I being pulled over? He gradually stopped on the shoulder, rolled down his window, and waited for the state trooper to approach.

"Good morning, sir." the young officer said. "May I have your license, registration, and insurance information, please?"

Before reaching inside the glove box, Buck noticed the trooper had his right hand resting on the handle of his holstered pistol. He guessed that the officer was being cautious. Buck decided not to show his NYPD badge because he wasn't looking for favorable treatment.

As Buck handed the trooper the requested papers, he asked, "Officer, do you mind telling me why you stopped me?"

"Yes, sir. You've got a broken tail light on the passenger side of your vehicle. I could write you a ticket, but since I'm in a good mood today, I'll let you off with a warning as long as you promise to get it repaired before dark. It's not a good idea to drive your vehicle at night with a broken tail light."

"Sorry, Officer, I wasn't aware of the problem. Thanks for bringing it to my attention, and I promise to get it repaired before the end of the day."

"You do that." After reviewing the information, the officer returned the papers and said, "Have a good day." He began to whistle, turned, and strolled back to his cruiser.

As Buck returned his papers to the glove box, he noticed his badge and Glock 19 pistol—the gun that had taken down Cheryl's killer.

The Glock 19 was a fifteen-round semi-automatic 9 mm pistol manufactured as a smaller version of the Glock 17. Its smaller size made it easier to grip and conceal, making it the choice of countless police departments worldwide. The pistol had saved his life on several occasions, and Buck hoped he would never have to use it again other than for target practice.

He decided to stop at the next exit, find a Chevrolet dealer, and get the tail light replaced. Buck didn't want to take a chance of getting stopped again because the next officer might not be as accommodating.

It took three hours before he could get back on the road. The first two dealers didn't have the parts. Fortunately, four exits down the highway, a third dealer stocked the parts and performed the repairs. Three hundred and fifty dollars lighter, Buck was back on I-95.

He had left New York at eight, originally planning on arriving in Orono around four that afternoon, but the delay pushed back his arrival time until after seven.

As he approached Orono, something new caught his attention. It was a large bronze plaque welcome sign. Curious, Buck pulled over and began to read.

WELCOME TO ORONO, MAINE

The town of Orono was settled in 1774 by European-American settlers, and it was named in honor of Chief Joseph Orono of the Penobscot Nation. Orono, with a population of approximately 9,500, is home to the University of Maine, with an enrollment of over 11,000 students. The university was founded in 1862 as part of the Morrill Act, signed by President Lincoln. In 1865 it was established as a land grant college. The university is situated on Marsh Island between the Penobscot and Stillwater rivers, with a campus of 660 acres. It is the largest university in the State of Maine.

Buck had planned to enroll at the University of Maine after high school. He had wanted to become a mechanical engineer, but that didn't become a reality due to unforeseen circumstances.

As he drove away, his thoughts returned to his high school days. As a teenager, he and his friends used to party on the banks of the Penobscot River in the summer. They would swim by day, light a bonfire at night, drink beer, and smoke pot.

He was madly in love with his high school sweetheart, Doreen

Warren. Doreen, a knockout, had long blonde hair, the bluest eyes he had ever seen, and a figure that drove all the boys wild.

Before Buck, Doreen dated Russell Sykes. Since middle school, everyone, including his parents, called him Rusty because of his reddish-orange hair.

Rusty lived in a trailer park community near Orono. His meek-mannered mother cleaned houses for affluent people in the area. His father worked as a handyman when he was sober. When he drank alcohol, he became violent and often beat his wife and Rusty for no good reason. Most nights, Rusty came home late to avoid the beatings, hoping his dad would be passed out and in bed. Rusty was a bit of a rebel and had a volatile temper. He always seemed to be getting into trouble with his teachers. Rusty smoked and sold pot to students and anyone who could afford to pay his price. Somehow, he always managed to avoid getting caught.

When Doreen's mother and father heard of Rusty's activities, they forbade her from going out with him. The day Doreen broke up with Rusty, he wasn't a happy camper.

Rusty liked to play Mr. Tough Guy in middle and high school. He picked on smaller kids that he knew he could beat up. Buck did not take kindly to Rusty's bullying and told him to pick on someone his size. That resulted in several fistfights between the two. Buck won most of the fights, which did not sit well with Rusty. When Buck started to date Doreen, Rusty became jealous and more hostile toward Buck. In high school, Buck beat out Rusty for the starting quarterback position. Rusty didn't like playing second fiddle as the backup quarterback. That was another reason he despised Buck.

Buck and Doreen were at the summer vacation party at the river one summer night after graduation. There must have been fifty or more teenagers whooping it up. Most of them were drunk, including Buck. A bonfire was roaring and shooting sparks into the heavens, and a few guys were playing guitars and singing rock songs.

Doreen and Buck got into an argument. He still remembers the angry look on her face when she screamed, "Buck Woods, you're drinking too much, and you're acting like a complete jerk."

As Doreen stomped off, Buck laughed and shouted, "I'm just having fun and letting off a little steam. Cut me some slack, will you? School's over, and it's time to party." He staggered into the woods to water the lilies.

When Buck returned, he could not find Doreen. At the time, Buck thought nothing of it. An hour went by, and he still hadn't spotted her. Buck asked his best friend, Jim Barkowsky, and his girlfriend, Shawna Clarkson, if they had seen Doreen, and they said they hadn't seen her in quite a while. That's when he began to panic. Buck asked everyone, and nobody had seen her. Because she was angry at him, he thought Doreen must have decided to go home alone.

Rusty Sykes and his new girlfriend, Brenda Blake, were there that night. He was up to his old shenanigans, smoking and selling pot. Since no love was lost between Rusty and Buck, they avoided one another.

After Doreen disappeared, Buck noticed that Rusty and Brenda had also vanished. He thought it was just a coincidence and never gave it a second thought.

When Doreen didn't come home that night, her parents began to worry. It was not like her to stay out all night. The following day Doreen's mother called Buck and asked if she had spent the night at his house. Buck sheepishly told her about their argument and said he thought Doreen had gone home alone. After checking with Doreen's best girlfriend and finding out she was not there, her parents became frantic. They went to the police, and a search began immediately.

That afternoon, they found Doreen's body floating downriver in shallow water near shore. She had a large bump and a gash on her forehead. After investigating, the police concluded that Doreen must have been walking too close to the water. They speculated that she had slipped, hit her head on a rock, and fallen into the river. With all the noise from the party, nobody claimed to have heard any screams for help. The police surmised that the fall had probably knocked Doreen unconscious. Not being a good swimmer, she would not have survived the river's strong current. The police questioned everyone who had attended the party, including Rusty, and no one claimed to have seen or heard a thing. Since there was no proof of foul play, the police had to rule Doreen's death was a tragic accident.

Buck gave Doreen a gold-plated necklace with a heart-shaped locket as a graduation gift. The engraving read, "To Doreen, Love Buck." She had been wearing it the night of the party, but when the police recovered her body, it was not around her neck. Buck wondered how the necklace had come off—was it buried in the mud at the bottom of the Penobscot River?

Three days later, Doreen's funeral was overflowing with mourners at St. Mary's Roman Catholic Church. Like zombies, Doreen's parents, Joan and Roy Warren attended their daughter's funeral in shock.

It was a sad and solemn service. The whole school attended—the one person missing was Rusty Sykes. When Buck had asked Brenda Blake why Rusty wasn't there, she said he was at home with the flu. To this day, Buck never believed her story.

After the funeral, Buck decided to escape all the bad memories. Feeling responsible for Doreen's death, he began to have nightmares about the night Doreen died. Despite his protesting parents, Buck changed his mind about attending university. The day after his eighteenth birthday Buck joined the Marines. Trained as a scout sniper, he spent four years serving his country. Severely wounded in the Gulf War, Buck spent several months recuperating at Bethesda Naval Hospital. When released, he received an honorable discharge and headed to New York City. After a break of one year, Buck applied to the NYPD. He was accepted, and after graduating from the police academy, over several years, he worked his way up the ladder from a patrol officer to a detective, starting on the drug squad and eventually filling an opening in the homicide division at the 52nd Precinct in the Bronx.

As he drove down Main Street, Buck's stomach growled louder than a starving grizzly. Spotting an empty parking space, he pulled in a short distance from Kelly's Bar & Grill. His throat felt as dry as the Sahara, and he longed for the thirst-quenching taste of an ice-cold beer and a steaming bowl of Kelly's delicious Irish stew.

Colin Kelly, the owner, had opened Kelly's Bar & Grill back in 1996. A talented musician, he played a mean guitar and was the lead singer in a band called the Shamrocks. About five years ago, the group felt it was time to hang up their instruments and retire. The Four-Leaf Clovers, a new Irish band of younger musicians from Bangor, replaced the Shamrocks.

As Buck walked through the door, the loud hum of people talking and laughing invaded his ears. The familiar sound of uptempo Irish music blasted from the wall-mounted speakers. He could barely hear himself think. Buck smiled; it felt good to be home again!

CHAPTER 3

Friday night, the end of the workweek, found the crowd in a festive mood and ready to party.

Buck slowly squeezed through the mass of humanity and reached the crowded bar. Standing behind an older man, he waved and caught the attention of the pretty blonde barmaid. He ordered a Bud Light, and while waiting for his beer, he looked around and spotted a few familiar faces.

Colin Kelly talked and laughed with another person he recognized as Steve Smith, Orono's mayor. Steve had been elected and re-elected as far back as Buck could recall. He wondered if Steve was that good or if maybe no one else wanted his job. Buck had to chuckle. He remembered Steve's slogan, "STEVE SMITH FOR HONEST GOVERNMENT." He wasn't sure Steve had an honest bone in his body, but so far, no one could prove otherwise. Steve was a likable fellow. He was Colin's good friend and the Shamrocks' former drummer.

Buck grabbed his beer and decided to work his way over and say hello. When he arrived, the two men abruptly ceased their conversation. Seeing Buck, surprised, Colin said, "The prodigal son returns. Buck Woods, it's great to see you! It's been a long time." He extended his hand. "What brings you back to town?"

Colin Kelly still had most of his Irish accent, having immigrated with his parents to the U.S. in his late teens. He stood about five feet nine inches tall, with a slim build and short gray hair. Colin always seemed to have a twinkle in his bright blue eyes.

Steve Smith slapped Buck on the back. "Good to see you, my boy. Welcome home." They shook hands.

Steve Smith looked the opposite of Colin Kelly. Short and overweight, he was completely bald. He sported a full gray beard, and his brown eyes were big and round. His face always seemed to carry a friendly politician's smile.

"Thanks, Mr. Mayor," Buck said. "It's good to see you both again. It's been several years since I was last home, and it feels good to be back."

Steve Smith was a typical politician, always looking for votes. If Buck had been a baby, Steve probably would have kissed him.

"I'm curious. What've you been doing all these years?" Colin asked. "The last time I spoke to your father, he said you were in New York City with the NYPD."

"That's right. I'm still there. When I left after high school, I enrolled in the Marines and spent four years with Uncle Sam. After the Marines, I joined the NYPD. It's hard to believe, but I've been there for almost twenty years. I'm a homicide detective at the 52nd Precinct. I had some time coming to me, so I've decided to take an extended vacation. I inherited my grandpa's cabin on Pushaw Lake several years ago when he passed away. I plan to renovate the cabin, settle in, and relax. If I get bored, I may retire from the NYPD and run for mayor in Orono's next election." Buck grinned.

Both men chuckled, and Steve Smith said, "That might be a good idea, Buck, because this will be my last term, and the town will be looking for fresh young talent."

"Yeah." Colin laughed, playfully poking Steve in the ribs. "It's time this old fart retired because we need young blood to bring fresh ideas to this old town."

"No thanks! I was kidding. Politics isn't my game, and I've had enough politics with the NYPD to last me a lifetime. If you two will excuse me, I'm starved. I'm dying for a bowl of your tasty Irish stew, Colin."

"It's still as good as ever," Colin said. "Enjoy! See you around, Buck."

Steve said, "It's been good seeing you again, Buck."

Buck worked his way through the crowd back to the bar. As he arrived, an elderly man said, "I've got to go. Would you like my seat?"

"Thanks," Buck said, "I appreciate it."

He sat down, waved the barmaid over, and ordered another beer and a bowl of stew.

When his food arrived, the mouth-watering smell of Irish stew invaded his nostrils. Buck dug in. He wolfed down his food quickly, mopping up the remaining gravy with freshly baked homemade sourdough bread. He took another pull on his beer, let out a stifled burp, and then a contented sigh.

Just as he had finished eating, Buck's head snapped forward from a hard slap on his back. Then someone gave him a big bear hug from behind. A familiar voice yelled, "B.J. Woods, you old devil, what the hell are you doin' here?"

He recognized the voice of his old high school pal, Jim Barkowsky. He enrolled in the Maine Criminal Justice Academy a few years after graduating high school. Jim had always said his goal was to become chief of the Orono Police Department. After several years as a patrol officer, Buck heard, through his father, that Jim was promoted to detective. He was the only detective on Orono's small police force.

Jim, three inches shorter than Buck, had started losing his hair in high school. Completely bald, he reminded Buck of Aristotelis "Telly" Savalas, the actor who played Kojak, the detective on the TV series. All Jim's friends called him "Telly."

Buck turned, stood up, and grinning from ear to ear, he put Jim in a headlock and rubbed his knuckles on his bald scalp.

"Ouch," Jim said with a laugh.

"Son of a bitch, if it ain't the old lawman himself, Detective Barkowsky. Guess I'd better behave myself, or you might throw my ass in jail. Come to think of it, I do need a place to crash, but I think the University Inn would be much more comfortable."

Jim grinned and said, "Don't rent a room, partner. You can bunk in at our house. Forget the University Inn. You're staying with us. I won't take no for an answer. Follow me. The band will be going on soon. In the meantime, we've got a lot of catching up to do."

Buck paid his tab and left a generous tip for the barmaid. He grabbed his beer and followed Jim, weaving in and out of the crowd. As they approached the stage, Buck saw Jim's wife, Shawna. She sat at a round, wooden table with four chairs, sipping red wine. In her early forties, her short caramel hair was perfectly styled, and her chocolate-brown eyes sparkled in the dimly lit room. Shawna had a smile that radiated like the noonday sun.

Her face lit up like a Christmas tree when she saw the two men. Shawna jumped to her feet and made a beeline for them. Ignoring Jim, she wrapped her arms around Buck's neck and kissed his cheek.

"Buck Woods," she hollered, "what a pleasant surprise! It's so nice to see you again. It seems a lifetime since you were last home."

Like most girls in high school, Shawna had a crush on Buck. Now, at age forty-two, he was still a good-looking man. In excellent condition, Buck ran most days and regularly worked out at a gym. His six-foot-three frame didn't have an ounce of fat. He had a full head of wavy black hair with a few streaks of gray, and his jade-green eyes still mesmerized the opposite sex.

Shawna smiled and said, "You're still as handsome as ever, Mr. Woods. You haven't aged a day since I last saw you."

Buck laughed. "I don't know about that. I try not to look into a mirror too often these days. Anyway, it's great to see you, Shawna. You're still as beautiful as ever. Having married this old fart," he nodded at Jim, "seems to have agreed with you. He's a lucky man. By the way, how are Kristina and Nicolas? I'm sure I wouldn't recognize them after all these years. As I recall, they were both good-looking kids. They definitely take after their mother."

Jim laughed. He faked a hurt look and said, "Thanks a lot, buddy. I always thought their good looks came from me."

"God, how time flies," Buck said. "The last time I came home was several years ago when I returned for my grandfather's funeral."

"Yeah," Jim said, "that's the last time I remember seeing you. You stayed a few days, and then you were gone. We didn't get a chance to catch up. Why don't we sit, toast, and celebrate our reunion?"

After a toast to good health and friendship, Jim said, "Shawna, I've invited Buck to stay with us. He was going to check in at the University Inn, but I told him no way."

"That's great! I agree with Jim, and there's no way you're staying in any hotel while you're in town, and we'd be insulted if you did. You're welcome to stay as long as you like."

"I don't want to put you guys out, but knowing you two, you won't take no for an answer. Thanks, I appreciate it."

Jim asked, "By the way, are you still a homicide detective with the NYPD?"

"For now, but I decided to take a six-month sabbatical. When Grandpa Woods died, I inherited his old cabin on Pushaw Lake. I didn't have time to do much about it until now, and I plan to renovate it and stay until October."

"That sounds great," Jim said.

"How's your dad doing in Florida?" Shawna asked.

Buck's mom, Mary, passed away in April 1995 after a two-year battle with ovarian cancer. Five years later, his dad, David, sold his accounting business at fifty-five, retired, and moved to Sarasota. He purchased a two-bedroom mobile home in a gated community with a small spring-fed lake and a private eighteen-hole golf course. David was an avid golfer. He didn't take long to fit in and make male and female friends. Buck called his dad at night because he always seemed to be out on the golf course during the day. He was pleased that his father seemed to be enjoying life again. Buck and his dad had never been close. His dad was strict but never abusive. David had always been respected and liked by his clients and friends. When Buck was a kid, his dad had spent long hours building his accounting business. During income tax season, he lived at his downtown office. Buck felt more of a bond with his grandfather, who took him fishing during summer vacation.

"He's doing fine. A few weeks ago, I returned from visiting him for two months. He took my mom's death hard, but all the sunshine and golfing worked miracles. He looks and sounds like his old self again, and he's even got a lady friend who loves to golf as much as he does."

"That's good to hear," Shawna said.

"When do you plan to start working on the cabin?" Jim asked.

"I'm heading out tomorrow morning to see what I need to do."

Excited, Jim said, "Hey, I'm off this weekend. If you don't mind, maybe I'll tag along. We could shoot the breeze and down a few beers, and it would be like old times."

"Sounds good, Jim. I look forward to it, and I might even put you to work," Buck said with a laugh.

A deep, sarcastic voice said, "Well, look who's here. Buckley, the asshole's back in town."

Buck glanced up and saw a large muscular man with a reddish-orange crewcut and a scowling face glaring down at him. It was his old childhood nemesis, Rusty Sykes.

Rusty had supposedly cleaned up his act after Doreen Warren's death. Deciding to become a police officer, he had taken his courses a few years after Jim. Upon graduation, Chief Durham hired him to replace a retiring officer. When the opening came up, Rusty applied for the detective job, showing his displeasure when Jim was chosen. Since Jim was a close friend of Buck's, Rusty also hated him. Neither of them went out of their way to be friendly.

Buck didn't like it when he was called Buckley. Whenever Rusty called him that, he hated the name and Rusty even more. The name reminded him of that horrible-tasting cough syrup his mother gave him as a kid. The only other person that had ever called him Buckley was his mother. As a kid, whenever he got into trouble, his mother would scold him and yell, 'Buckley John Woods, what were you thinking, or stop that, right now!' Like Jim, his dad and a few close friends usually called him Buck or B.J.

Instantly enraged, Buck jumped to his feet. Standing toe to toe and face to face with fists clenched, the two men glared at one another, waiting to see who would blink first. In a calm voice, Buck said, "Well, hello to you too, Rusty. If you want to know, I came back to piss you off and to beat the shit out of you, just like in the old days."

Daggers flew from Rusty's eyes, and with a menacing scowl, he said, "You and what fuckin' army, Buckley?"

Buck laughed and said, "Let's take this outside, and you'll see I don't need a fucking army. And don't call me Buckley, you idiot."

"A little sensitive, aren't we? Okay, Buckley. Sorry, I mean asshole," Rusty said with a smirk.

Before things escalated further, Jim promptly squeezed between them and pushed the two men apart. "Hey, calm down, guys. Let's not go off the deep end here." With his dry humor, he said, "This isn't the time or place to renew your friendship."

People were beginning to stare. Hearing the commotion, Rusty's wife, Brenda, rushed over, grabbed him by the arm, and said, "Come on, Rusty. You've had way too much to drink. Leave Buck alone. It's time to go. Sorry, Buck."

"Don't apologize to that asshole," Rusty screamed as she pulled him away.

Buck's eyes narrowed, and with a cold, icy glare, he shouted back, "Saved by the bell again, eh, Sykes?"

Rusty turned and yelled, "This ain't over by a long shot. See you soon, Buckley!"

When Rusty and Brenda were gone, Shawna asked, "What the hell was that all about?"

Buck grinned and said, "Apparently, Rusty still hates my guts. He can't seem to forget the past. I suppose I'm just as bad. I like pushing his buttons and hate when he calls me Buckley. We've been having a feud since we were kids in middle school. He'd bully smaller kids like Terry Wells, I'd stick up for them, and Rusty and I would always end up fighting. I won most of the fights, making him even angrier."

"Yeah," Jim laughed, "I remember he was pissed when you beat him out in high school for the starting quarterback position. When Doreen Warren broke up with him, he went nuts when she started dating you. Rusty always wants to be first in everything. He can't stand losing. When I got the detective job, Rusty openly displayed hostility toward me. He thought he was going to get it. Rusty's nose has been out of joint ever since, and his attitude toward me has been anything but cordial. You being my friend doesn't help. I don't think he has any friends, and most people at the station try to stay out of his way. I'm surprised he hasn't been fired by now. I think Chief Durham feels sorry for him because of his family situation, having been brought up by an abusive father. Unfortunately, Rusty's a product of his environment and always seems to have a chip on his shoulder. He thinks the whole world is out to get him. Chief Durham is patient and tolerant, but one day Rusty will push too far. In my opinion, he's a time bomb waiting to explode."

"I agree," Buck said. "You certainly don't want to turn your back on him."

A smile blossomed on Shawna's face, and with a mischievous twinkle in her eyes, she said, "You grown men are worse than little boys. Why can't you get along and play nice?"

Just then, the band started to play. Shawna grabbed Buck by the hand and pulled him onto the dance floor.

CHAPTER 4

By the time they closed Kelly's, Buck's blood pressure had returned to normal. When they arrived at Jim and Shawna's, he had calmed down, his confrontation with Rusty all but forgotten.

The Barkowsky residence sat on nine wooded acres four miles from downtown Orono. The gray brick two-story, four-bedroom house had an impressive front porch and a detached three-car garage. The home was immaculate and well-maintained.

Jim helped Buck with his bags while Shawna led them into the clean guest room that contained a three-piece ensuite bathroom.

"Goodnight, Buck, my friend," Jim said. "See you in the morning."

"Sleep tight, Buck," Shawna said as she kissed him on the cheek and left.

"Goodnight, you two, and thanks again for your hospitality. See you in the morning."

The next morning, at the kitchen table, Buck and Jim were tired and hung over.

After Shawna had prepared a delicious breakfast of freshly squeezed orange juice, bacon, scrambled eggs, toast, and steaming coffee, the two men felt human again. They were sipping their second cup of coffee as they talked over old times when Kristina and Nicolas, still sleepy, joined them.

Since they had stayed at Kelly's until closing time, Buck had not had a chance to see the kids.

As they entered the room, Buck jumped to his feet and gave Kristina a big hug and a kiss on the cheek. He shook hands with Nicolas and hugged him, lifting him off his feet.

"God," he said, "I still pictured you as kids, and I can hardly believe how grown-up you two are."

Kristina had long dark hair, stood a little over five feet, and was pretty, just like her mother. She had bright, round dark-brown eyes and a warm, friendly smile. Kristina had always been a little shy and blushed when Buck hugged her.

Nicolas was a handsome young man. He stood close to six feet tall, with dark curly hair and a muscular build. He, too, had brown eyes and a noticeable dimple on his right cheek when he smiled.

Last night, Jim told Buck that Nicolas played hockey, football, and lacrosse and was a Boston Bruins, Patriots, and Red Sox fan. Kristina had been a local figure skating club member since she was six. Over the years, she had competed and won several gold, silver, and bronze medals in state and out-of-state competitions. Kristina taught figure skating part-time while attending the University of Maine. Completing her second year of Marine Biology, she would be finished for the summer in a few weeks.

They seemed a little shy at first, but after Buck asked a few questions about school and sports, they opened up and would not stop talking. Buck sat back and enjoyed every minute of their conversation, especially when they called him uncle Buck.

Buck asked, "What are your plans for the summer?"

Kristina could hardly contain her excitement as she told him about her summer job. The State of Maine Health and Environmental Testing Lab had hired her. They provided Kristina with a car to drive around and gather samples of lake and river water throughout the state. The lab would test for pollutants to ensure the water was safe where people swam.

Nicolas said that his summer job wasn't as exciting. He would be stocking shelves and doing odd jobs at the local IGA grocery store.

Jim interrupted. "Hey guys, you've talked Uncle Buck's ears off. It's time to give him a break. We have to go to his cabin, so save some for later, okay."

Buck offered to help clean up, but Shawna wouldn't have any

part of it. She told them to get going and do their man thing. Jim and Buck grabbed their coats, said goodbye, and headed out the door.

They took Buck's truck and, on the way, stopped at a convenience store. Jim picked up a six-pack of Bud Light and a bag of ice, and he placed the beer into a small red plastic cooler he had brought and dumped in the ice.

Less than twenty minutes later, they turned into the overgrown laneway of Buck's new home. When he stopped at the back door, he whistled softly. He could see the shingles were starting to crumble and curl. They left the truck and walked to the front of the cabin overlooking the lake. The porch floorboards showed signs of rotting, and the support posts leaned in different directions.

Buck turned to Jim and said, "If the outside is this bad, I can only imagine how the inside must look."

Jim laughed and said, "Yeah, B.J., this project is bound to keep you out of mischief for a while."

Buck chuckled and said, "I don't mind a little hard work, but this place looks like a disaster. It reminds me of the house in the movie, The Money Pit."

Jim noticed Buck smiling as he stared at the rotting front porch. "A penny for your thoughts," he said.

"I was thinking about how time flies. Man, this place brings back fond memories. As a kid, I'd stay here for a week or two during summer vacation. Grandpa Woods would take me fishing in his old wooden rowboat. We'd fish all day, and after cleaning the fish we caught, we'd sit on this porch and enjoy the great view. Grandpa would sip on a beer while I drank a soda. I enjoyed listening to his fish stories. I think he'd exaggerate the size of the fish by several inches or more. Grandpa would hold his arms apart three or more feet and tell me about the big one he caught and the bigger one that got away. He laughed and told me he might have pulled my leg a little. Grandma would fry up the fish and cook great meals. After dinner, I'd be so tired I'd go to bed early and sleep like a log. The next morning, Grandpa would shake me to get up at six, and we'd do it again. The cabin was almost new back then, and Grandpa always kept it pristine. Those were happy times. It's sad to see how neglected it is now. My goal is to make it look like it did back then."

"Oh, well," Jim said, "when you're done sprucing it up, I'm sure it'll look new again."

They had to watch their step on the porch for fear of falling through and twisting an ankle or breaking a leg.

When Buck pulled out his key to open the padlock, it took a split second to realize someone had used a hacksaw to cut through it.

"Guess I won't need this key," Buck said. The tired, rusty hinges squeaked as he shoved the door open. "Remind me to oil or replace the hinges. On second thought, maybe I'll buy a new door."

With Jim on his heels, they entered directly into the living room. The stench was so foul that they both started to gag and retch. Turning around, they retreated to the porch, where they both doubled over and brought up Shawna's sumptuous breakfast. After inhaling and exhaling several deep breaths of fresh air, they began to feel much better.

Buck said, "What the hell was that awful smell? Before we attempt to go back in, I think I need a beer."

"That sounds like one hell of a good idea," Jim agreed.

They returned to the truck, opened the cooler, and grabbed a beer. "Ah, that feels better," Buck said after guzzling half the bottle.

Jim chuckled. "There's nothing like an ice-cold beer to help settle an upset stomach."

"If I had to take a guess, I'd say the stench in the cabin is decomposed flesh. Maybe a raccoon up and died of old age," Buck laughed. "In my job, I've dealt with tons of dead bodies over the years, and the stink of decomposing flesh smells similar to what we just experienced."

"Well, it sure doesn't smell like Betty Crocker's fresh-baked cookies," Jim quipped.

"You got that right, Telly."

They both laughed briefly, then, looking at one another, turned deadly serious.

Buck said, "When I was in the Gulf War, we came across bodies that had been dead for only a few days. In that heat, the stench was unbearable, and my stomach never got used to it."

"I'll take your word for it, my friend. Around here, we rarely run into that sort of thing. I remember, a few years ago, when old Charlie 'The Hermit' Clark died, his body wasn't discovered for a week, and man, he was ripe. I was called to the scene to ensure foul play wasn't involved. That was the first time I smelled anything so awful, and I emptied my stomach on the spot. I couldn't eat much or sleep for days. His decomposed body and the stench kept flashing through my head."

Buck said, "We'd better find out what happened inside. Before going back, we'll need something to cover our noses."

Buck entered the storage shed and found a few rags that looked clean. He shook out the dust, and each man tied a rag around his nose and mouth. Looking like a couple of bank robbers from the old west, they decided to try it again.

This time, Jim led the way. Breathing through their mouths, they checked the living room—nothing. Next, they checked the kitchen and the bathroom—nothing. The first bedroom looked undisturbed. When they entered the master bedroom, they found the source of the rotten egg smell that had engulfed the entire cabin. His head was in a dried pool of blood, lying face up on the floor beside the bed. With a bullet hole in the middle of his forehead, he stared at the ceiling with unseeing eyes. There was no gun or shell casing near the body.

From experience, Buck guessed that the man had been dead for at least a week, maybe longer. He looked to be between forty and fifty years of age. A few maggots crawled in and around his mouth.

"Gross," Jim said. "Look at those fucking maggots."

"Let's get the hell outta here," Buck said as bile began to creep into his throat.

Once more, they started to gag and retch. Bolting to the door, they jumped over the rotting porch and landed hard on the ground.

Taking off their improvised masks, they breathed in the relief of fresh air. Walking to the truck, they opened another beer, sank to the ground, and guzzled until the bottles were empty.

With sweat dripping off his forehead, Jim said, "We have a dead body inside, but how did he get here? Where's his vehicle? Did the killer or killers take it? I'm sure he didn't walk to your cabin."

"The ground is hard and dry, and there don't appear to be tire tracks," Buck said. "If he had a vehicle, there aren't any signs I can see."

Jim said, "I'd better call this in. We'll need an officer out here with a log book and crime-scene tape. The Criminal Investigation Division of the Maine State Police and the Maine Attorney General's Office must be notified. They'll probably assign a detective from the Maine State Police to work with me on the investigation. In the meantime, all we can do is sit tight and secure the crime scene. I hope we didn't disturb any evidence."

Buck noticed that Jim's police training had kicked in, and he was now thinking like a detective in command of a homicide investigation.

Killing time waiting for the authorities to arrive, Buck asked, "I'm curious, Telly, how large is the Orono PD compared to when we were teenagers? I imagine it must have grown a little since those days."

"Yeah, B.J., I think it's a bit bigger. The Administrative Division consists of Chief John Durham, Captain Tony Timpano, and Administrative Assistant Elsie Brody. The chief and the captain are responsible for the management and supervision of the department, while Elsie takes care of the secretarial, clerical, and record-keeping duties. She also looks after administration for the Orono Fire Department in the same building. The Patrol Division has three sergeants and twelve patrol officers. There's a School Resource Officer, a Services Volunteer Coordinator, and a chaplain—lucky me, I'm the only detective. We're just a little smaller than the NYPD," Jim said.

Buck grinned and said, "Yeah, it's a little smaller. Not by much— the NYPD has between thirty-four and thirty-five thousand cops."

It took forty-five minutes for a young officer named Craig Walker to arrive. He handed Jim a logbook and a roll of crime scene tape. After Jim introduced him to Buck, Craig and Jim sealed off the area around the front and rear entrances. When they finished, Craig headed back to town.

It took three hours for the State Police forensic team to arrive. As they piled out of the long white van, Jim recognized everyone.

Dr. Corey Chambers, the medical examiner, was the head of the crime lab. She had a medical degree with a specialty in forensic pathology. Corey, closing in on forty, was slightly overweight. She had a brown ponytail and blue eyes and stood about five feet four. Despite her job, Dr. Chambers had a dry sense of humor and always seemed in a good mood.

Photographer Dan Evans, a good-looking young man in his mid-twenties, had short blond hair and a medium build. His baby face made him look younger than his actual age.

The third member of the team, Doug Graham, the fingerprint expert, looked athletic and in his mid-thirties. He was about six feet tall, with sandy brown hair and a neatly trimmed beard covering his round face.

Shortly after the forensic team, Paul Prentice, Assistant DA, arrived, followed by Detective Brad Strongman from the Maine State Police.

Prentice had movie-star good looks, and he stood just over six feet and appeared to be in his mid-forties. His short, cropped black hair had a few streaks of gray, and his face was clean-shaven. When he smiled, his straight white teeth gleamed like a model in a toothpaste commercial.

Detective Brad Strongman was a veteran of the Maine State Police force. He was a tall, slim man in his early fifties with short-cropped gray hair, piercing blue eyes, a long, thin nose, and a pointed jaw.

As he exited his car, Jim whispered to Buck, "That's Brad Strongman from the Maine State Police. I worked on a case with him a few years ago, and we didn't hit it off. I found Strongman to be arrogant and bullheaded. He thinks he knows everything, and I dread working with him again."

"It sounds like he's a real jerk, but you might want to give him the benefit of the doubt. Maybe he's changed," Buck whispered back.

"Fat chance—don't think so, once a jerk, always a jerk," Jim whispered.

Spotting Jim, Brad Strongman walked straight up to him and extended his hand. Like a long-lost friend, he said, "Jim, it looks like we'll be on this case together. I look forward to working with you again."

They shook hands.

"Hello, Brad. It's nice to see you again, and I look forward to it, too," Jim lied.

He introduced Buck to Brad Strongman and everyone else as his friend and the property owner. He also mentioned that Buck was on vacation from his job as an NYPD homicide detective. They all shook hands and exchanged polite greetings.

Jim said, "Buck and I came to check his property to see what repairs are needed. When we arrived, we discovered the body of a Caucasian male lying on the master bedroom floor. There's a bullet hole in his forehead; no weapon or shell casing was found near the body. All signs indicate that the victim was murdered. By the way, Paul, you won't have to worry about getting a search warrant before the forensic team searches the place. As the owner, Buck has consented to do what is necessary to obtain any evidence to help find the killer."

"That's good news, Jim. Thanks, Buck, that'll save a lot of time."

Ignoring Jim, Brad Strongman asked, "Well, Buck, since you're a fellow homicide detective, what's your take on the crime scene?"

"As Jim said, I'm a vacationing homicide detective, and I'd like it to stay that way. I'd rather not speculate, so I'll leave that up to you and Jim. I prefer to keep my nose out of it."

"Okay, Buck, I understand. It's not a good way to start a vacation," Strongman said.

Jim smiled. Buck's answer pleased him.

Dan Evans said, "I'm going to start taking pictures."

He photographed the front and rear entrances, taking close-up shots of the damaged lock. Then he retraced his steps and filmed the areas he had just photographed.

After the crew had logged in, Dr. Corey Chambers handed out masks, bootie covers, long-sleeved gowns, and latex gloves to everyone before entering the cabin. The gowns and masks looked similar to those used in operating rooms. Once they were ready, she led the way.

Not officially part of the investigation team, Buck remained outside. He returned to his truck, tilted his seat back, and closed his eyes. He hoped to get a little shut-eye to catch up on some of the sleep he'd lost the previous night.

The team followed Dr. Chambers as she entered the cabin. She carried a notepad and a pen, ready to take notes along the way.

The masks helped, but the stench was still overwhelming.

Dr. Chambers laughed and said, "It would've been better if we had brought gas masks. We'll do a walk-through a few times to understand what happened here. Follow my lead, and please try not to disturb anything."

The walk-through is to explore the scene and to get an idea of the nature of the crime. Such things as how the crime was committed, the point of entry, the point of exit, and any signs of a struggle would help to determine what needed to be more closely examined and what evidence, if any, might be present. They repeated the tour one more time to make sure nothing was missed.

"It doesn't look like anyone has lived here for a long time," Paul Prentice said, pointing to the cobwebs that hung from the overhead light fixtures. Dust covered most surfaces.

"It's been quite a while," Jim said. "Buck's grandfather passed away several years ago, and no one's lived here since then. Now that Buck's on vacation, he's planning to restore and update the cabin."

The worn-out brown living room sofa and threadbare red recliner appeared in their original positions, facing the fieldstone fireplace on the right-hand wall. The fireplace didn't show any signs of recent use. The eat-in kitchen adjoined the living room. A back door off the kitchen led to the parking area. It appeared as if the wooden kitchen table had been wiped clean. A green glass ashtray containing several cigarette butts sat in the middle of the table. Nothing seemed to be broken, indicating that a struggle had not occurred.

"Judging by the cigarette butts in the ashtray, someone's been here recently. They even swept the floor to eliminate any footprints in the dust. It's funny; I don't see a broom or dustpan anywhere," Strongman said.

When they entered the bathroom, Dr. Chambers said, "It looks like we've got dirty bedsheets and soiled pillowcases in the bathtub."

Buck tried, but he couldn't nap. All his years as a homicide detective kept his mind active. He was trying to figure out who the dead man could be and how he ended up in his cabin. Wild thoughts flashed through his brain.

Was the man a homeless person who was using the cabin for shelter? That seemed highly unlikely. His plaid shirt, jeans, and boots all appeared relatively new, not the typical attire of a vagrant. Who would want to kill a homeless person, anyway? It sure wouldn't be for his money!

Was he a drug dealer shot by a partner after a disagreement? Was it a drug deal gone bad? Was he a gang member who wanted out and was trying to hide? Was he an undercover agent who had been exposed and executed by the Mafia, a drug dealer, or a gang?

Buck's imagination ran wild, considering all the possibilities. He had to keep reminding himself that he was on sabbatical to escape murder scenes. He had to stop thinking like a detective and let the local authorities solve the crime.

Dan Evans snapped pictures of every room. When he reached the master bedroom, he went to work. First, Dan snapped pictures of the room from every angle and took photos of the body. He took several close-ups of the face and the bullet hole in the man's forehead, hands, and shoes. He repeated the same procedure with his video camera. Dan didn't miss a thing.

It was clear from the unmade bed that someone had slept in it recently. The pillows and the bed sheets looked clean and in new condition, which explained the bed sheets and pillowcases in the bathroom. A closer examination revealed stains on the mattress's bedsheet, and Dr. Chambers suspected the stains were semen from the victim. She removed the sheet and collected several blonde hairs as evidence from a pillow for DNA testing.

Doug Graham kept himself busy dusting the cabin for fingerprints. Jim had already forewarned him that Buck's prints would likely be on the front door and padlock.

When Dan had finished snapping pictures of the crime scene, Doug went to work fingerprinting the victim, after which he placed paper bags over the dead man's hands.

Dr. Chambers searched the body for identification but found nothing. The victim's left wrist and ring finger showed a white circle where a watch and ring were missing.

Dr. Chambers said, "It looks like whoever shot the victim must have taken his ID, credit cards, money, watch, and ring. Dental records might be the only way to identify the body. For now, he'll be called John Doe."

"I've seen a lot of homicides where robbery was the primary motive," Strongman said. "My sixth sense tells me that's not the case here. It looks like the shooter wants us to think that, and I feel it goes much deeper than that."

"I agree," Paul Prentice said. "It looks like there was more going on here than meets the eye. I'm glad I don't have to solve this one. I'll let you two detectives follow the clues, find the killer, and bring me a solid case to prosecute."

They decided to do a thorough search of the murder room. While looking under the bed, Jim found a .38 caliber shell casing. "It must have rolled there after the shot was fired," Jim said. "For some reason, the killer failed to pick it up. Was the killer in a hurry? Well, at least we know a .38 caliber gun killed the victim, and ballistics should confirm this when they test it against the slug."

With a smirk, Brad Strongman said, "That's obvious, Jim. You don't have to be a rocket scientist to figure that out."

Jim was fuming inside but held his tongue and ignored the jab.

Dr. Chambers labeled the shell casing and placed it inside a paper evidence bag.

"I'm sure we'll find the slug and casing will match when we do the autopsy," Dr. Chambers said.

There were six cigarette butts in the ashtray. Two of the butts had lipstick stains on the filter. The butts were collected and bagged. The DNA from the butts could help identify the killer.

After all the evidence had been gathered and labeled, Doug and Dan wrapped the corpse in a white sheet and placed it in a body bag. Dr. Chamber zipped and locked the bag, and the victim was lifted onto a gurney. Taking care not to fall through the rotting front porch, they wheeled the body out to the van. The corpse would be taken to the State Police Crime Lab in Augusta for an autopsy. Once identified, a death certificate will be issued, and the body, released to a funeral home of the next of kin's choosing.

"After the autopsy, when the evidence is analyzed, I'll forward a report to you and Brad, Jim," Dr. Chambers said.

"I look forward to receiving it," Jim said.

"Me, too," Strongman said.

After everyone had said goodbye, the forensic team piled into the van, honked the horn, and drove off, followed by Paul Prentice and Brad Strongman.

Before heading home, Jim turned to Buck and said, "I'll arrange for a crew to come out Monday morning to clean and sanitize the cabin. After they're done, you might want to put a new lock on the front door."

"Okay, I'll take care of it. I don't think there'll be any problem leaving the cabin unlocked, and it's not like there's anything valuable to steal."

"I don't think you'll have to worry about that," Jim agreed.

"Well, my friend, it's been quite a day. I could use a stiff drink or two," Buck said.

"Sounds like a plan. I'm not looking forward to working this case with that arrogant son of a bitch, Brad Strongman. A few stiff drinks might help to get that thought off my mind."

CHAPTER 5

When they arrived back at the house, no one was home. They headed to the family room, and Jim went to the wet bar. He threw some ice into a couple of glasses and poured two shots of whiskey. He handed one to Buck and said, "After the day we've had, we both need to sit down and unwind."

"I agree," Buck said.

They clinked glasses and swallowed the whiskey in one gulp. Jim poured another, and this time they sipped leisurely, savoring the smooth taste.

Buck said, "I've been trying to figure out what happened at the cabin and who the victim could be. Do you have any theories?"

"I think it could be a lovers' quarrel or a jealous husband who found his cheating wife and shot her lover."

"If that's the case, why didn't he shoot her too?"

"Maybe he did kill her, but not at the cabin. If he had left her body with her lover, chances are we'd be able to identify her and therefore identify him. We'll have to follow the clues and see where they lead," Jim said.

A moment later, the front door opened, and Shawna, Nicolas, and Kristina walked in.

"Hello," Shawna yelled.

"We're in the family room," Jim shouted back.

Shawna said as she entered the room, "I see you two got home safe and sound. How did it go?"

Jim said, "Don't even ask. You probably wouldn't believe me if I told you."

Shawna's eyes widened. "Now you've got me curious."

Just then, Kristina and Nicolas joined them.

"I think you all need to sit down," Jim said.

When they were sitting, he began to tell the story. After he finished, Kristina said, "God, it all sounds so spooky. Nothing like that ever happens around here. Uncle Buck, are you going to help Dad solve the murder?"

"No, Kristina, that's your dad's and Detective Brad Strongman's job. I work for the NYPD, and I don't think the Orono Police Department or the Maine State Police would appreciate my involvement in their case. Besides, I'm on vacation and intend to stay that way. Your dad and Detective Strongman don't need my help."

Nicolas chimed in. "Dad, who could've done such a horrible thing?"

"I don't have any idea, but that's what I intend to find out, with or without Brad Strongman."

After Shawna and the kids had retired for the night, the two men sat in the family room sipping whiskey. They had already consumed several drinks, and Jim could see that Buck was starting to relax and loosen up.

Jim asked, "How are you feeling, B.J.? You were coming home to relax and ended up with a dead body in your cabin and all the drama of a homicide investigation. I'm sure it must all be a little upsetting."

"I came home to work on the cabin, thinking it would be good therapy. I was hoping it would get my mind off a few things that have been bothering me. I didn't know how I'd feel after all these years. Coming back hasn't changed much. As you know, Doreen's death shook me up. I always felt I was responsible for what happened to her. I keep thinking she'd still be alive if I hadn't gotten drunk and had that argument with her. After her funeral, I couldn't face staying in Orono with all those terrible memories. Like a coward, I ran. By joining the Marines, I thought it would help me forget the past, but that didn't happen."

"You're too hard on yourself, partner. It wasn't your fault, and you can't go through life blaming yourself. No matter what you do, you can't bring Doreen back."

"I know, but I still have nightmares about Doreen's death. I've tried all sorts of things, from sleeping pills to booze and even therapy."

"I know you must be going through hell, Buck. I heard you cry out in your sleep last night, and you called out Doreen's name several times."

Looking embarrassed, Buck said, "Shit, I hope I didn't wake up the whole house."

"Don't worry about it. No one heard but me," Jim lied. "Before your father moved to Florida, he told me you were severely wounded during the Gulf War. He mentioned that you spent several months recuperating at Bethesda Naval Hospital."

"I was hoping he wouldn't have said anything. But now that the cat's out of the bag, I'd appreciate it if you'd keep it between us unless you've spilled the beans."

"Sorry, the only person I mentioned it to was Shawna, and I told her to keep it to herself. Knowing her, I'm sure she hasn't told anyone."

"I hope not. In 1991, during the Gulf War, a bullet missed my heart and vital organs by a fraction. Like a dummy, I wasn't wearing my vest. The doctors weren't sure if I would make it, and I lost so much blood that they had to give me several blood transfusions. Looking back, I almost wish I had died. Maybe I'd be with Doreen and wouldn't have all the guilt and agony that still consumes me."

"Buddy, you know Shawna, and I are here for you. If there's anything we can do, say the word."

"Thanks, I appreciate that."

Jim took a sip of his drink. He leaned forward and said, "Please continue, Buck; I'd like to hear the rest of your story."

"During my stay at Bethesda, they did some tests. I was diagnosed with PTSD. Fortunately, I had a good shrink. His name was Dr. Jonas Banner. He helped me through a lot of shit. I had flashbacks of combat and relived memories of traumatic events. I had trouble concentrating. My nerves were always on edge, and I'd have angry outbursts and aggressive behavior. I had negative feelings about myself and others and was a complete wreck. I hated sleeping because of all the recurring nightmares. I even contemplated suicide a few times but never got around to it. After six months of intensive therapy, according to Dr. Banner, I had made amazing progress. He pronounced me fit to be released with the caveat that I would probably still have nightmares occasionally. He felt the nightmares would gradually disappear as I returned to society and focused on other things. I still get them, but not as often as before. I suppose that's a positive sign. I obtained an honorable discharge at twenty-two when I was released. During my four years in the Marines, I saved enough money to last a while. I headed to New York City and spent a year unwinding. I went to several Broadway plays, Yankees, Mets, and Knicks games, and I even took in a few hockey games when the Rangers played the Islanders. Over the years, I've dated some beautiful and intelligent women. I came close to tying the knot once, but that's another story better left for another time. By the end of the year, I got bored and decided it was time to find a job, so I applied to the NYPD. After passing a few tests, I qualified, and they accepted me into the training program. When I graduated from the police academy, I was assigned to the 52nd Precinct in the Bronx. I pounded the beat as a rookie cop for two years, then graduated to a patrol car with a partner. A few years later, I made detective, starting on the drug squad. I was there for three years. When an opening came up on the homicide squad, I applied and got the job. I've been there ever since."

"Why did you become a cop after leaving the Marines?"

"I've always had a burning desire to protect people from bad things. I guess that's why I always took the side of the underdog—guys like Terry Wells, who couldn't protect themselves from bullies like Rusty Sykes. By joining the Marines, I was helping to protect the country I love, and by joining the NYPD, I could serve and protect my fellow citizens. Does any of this make sense?"

"It sure does, partner. I can relate to what you're saying. I joined the Orono PD for similar reasons. So far, I haven't regretted being in law enforcement a single day. I hope you don't think I'm prying. Do you mind if I ask why you decided to take a sabbatical? I suspect there might be more to it than just coming home to renovate the cabin."

"You're very perceptive, Telly." Buck laughed. "I guess that's why you became a detective. My excuse for getting away from NYC is coming home to fix the cabin, and I'm hoping manual labor will help get my mind off a few things. Last December, my partner, Cheryl Jenkins, married with two young daughters, was shot and killed. We were across the street having a coffee when we heard two gunshots. A young male suspect with a gun in his hand ran out of a convenience store after killing the female clerk during a robbery that went bad."

Buck went on to tell Jim about the pursuit. He told him how his partner was ambushed and how he shot and killed the suspect.

"At her funeral, seeing her two little girls and husband devastated told me it was time to get away before I got someone else killed. After Cheryl's funeral, the nightmares started again, so I had a few sessions with an NYPD shrink. The nightmares seemed to stop for a while, but I still get the odd one."

"Shit, B.J., it sounds like you've been to hell and back between Doreen's death, the Gulf War, and your partner's death. That's more tragedy than one person should endure in a lifetime. You can't blame yourself, Buck. Neither Doreen's nor Cheryl's death were your fault."

"You may be right, but I still feel responsible for their deaths, and I think hell would've been preferable," Buck said with a forced laugh. "Don't get me wrong. I'm not complaining, and I don't feel sorry for myself. I've got plenty to be thankful for, especially having great friends like you and Shawna."

"Buck, you know Shawna and I will always be your friends, and we'll always be here for you, come hell or high water. You're like the brother I never had."

"The feeling's mutual, my friend. By the way, I'd like to apologize to you and Shawna for not keeping in touch over the last several years, but I was in no shape to be social with anyone. For many years, whenever I looked in the mirror, I hated the person I saw. I still think about some of the things Dr. Banner did to help me get through my PTSD, and the NYPD shrink helped me to deal with Cheryl's death. Today, when I look in the mirror, the guy I see is beginning to smile again," Buck said, yawning and stretching.

"God, partner, there's no need to apologize. Now that I know what you've been through, I understand completely. I'm the one who should be apologizing to you, and I should have contacted you a long time ago. I appreciate you sharing your story with me. Are you ready to call it a night?"

"Sorry to bore you with all my problems, Telly. I don't know what got into me. It must be the booze. I haven't talked this much since I can't remember when."

"You didn't bore me, Buck. I'm glad you opened up and told me about all the shit you've been going through. I know it wasn't easy, and sometimes it helps to get things off your chest."

"I feel embarrassed having told you about my crappy life, but I'm relieved." Buck laughed, saying, "If you hear me screaming in my sleep, now you'll know why."

"Don't be embarrassed. I'm glad you feel better, having told me. And don't worry about screaming in your sleep. We all sleep like rocks, and I doubt anyone will hear you."

Jim stood up, went over to Buck, and hugged him tightly. When they separated, both men had tears in their eyes.

After Buck went to bed, Jim poured himself another drink and sat in his recliner, mulling over all the things Buck had said. Was he still suffering from PTSD? I hope not, but the nightmares are not a good sign. I think I'd better keep a close eye on him.

While Jim sat in the family room thinking about their conversation, Buck had another nightmare. This time it was not about Doreen or Cheryl. He was on a rooftop in Kuwait City with his trusted sniper rifle and another sniper nicknamed Tex. Their job was to protect a convoy of U.S. Marines entering the city. The convoy was less than a hundred yards from their position when an Iraqi soldier ran into the street. Before Buck or Tex could react, the soldier fired a shoulder-mounted anti-tank missile. It blew the armored vehicle to smithereens. Buck sighted the target and killed the soldier instantly, but he was too late. He left his position and galloped down the stairs to the street. When he arrived at the scene, he found what was left of five Marines. Buck hadn't noticed another Iraqi soldier leap from the same doorway. He fired his weapon, and the bullet penetrated Buck's chest, narrowly missing his heart. Tex killed the soldier, ran down, dragged Buck to safety, and called for a medic. The medic managed to ease the bleeding temporarily. Buck was airlifted to a field hospital, where doctors gave him several pints of blood during an operation that saved his life. A few days later, he woke up in Bethesda Naval Hospital in Bethesda, Maryland.

Before he went to bed, at two a.m., Jim had downed three more drinks, leaving the whiskey bottle bone dry. As he staggered past Buck's bedroom, he could swear he heard him mumbling in his sleep.

CHAPTER 6

Monday morning Jim was up early. He needed a strong black coffee to help clear the fog from his aching head. On his way to work, he stopped at the Verve and picked up a coffee and a couple of bagels. Jim was still trying to understand what had happened at Buck's cabin when administrative assistant Elsie Brody stuck her head through the doorway. She smiled and said, "Good morning, Jim. I hear you had an interesting weekend."

Jim returned her smile. "Good morning, Elsie. Yeah, a little more exciting than most weekends, and it's amazing how fast bad news travels."

Elsie had been with the department for as long as Jim could remember. In her mid-fifties, she always seemed to have a smile on her face. Her hair was wavy, long, and gray, and she had a slender nose and friendly sky-blue eyes. Elsie was a dedicated employee and the chief's right-hand woman.

A few minutes after Elsie had left, Chief of Police John Durham walked in. The chief was a good-looking man at age sixty-one, with a full head of snow-white hair and a wrinkle-free face. He stood about six feet tall and appeared in good physical condition.

"Good morning, Jim."

"Good morning, Chief."

"Could you please join me in my office for a minute?"

Jim picked up his coffee and followed the chief to his office.

Chief Durham motioned for him to sit. He smiled and said, "Sounds like you had a bit of a wild Saturday, Jim."

"You can say that again, Chief. Not your typical quiet Orono weekend."

"So, what do you think happened at Buck's cabin?"

Jim paused for a moment to gather his thoughts, and then he proceeded to tell the story. He mentioned the theory that the murder might have been a lovers' quarrel or a jealous husband finding his wife in bed with another man. He told the chief about their gathered evidence and that he was waiting on the ME's report.

When he finished, the chief said, "Sounds logical, Jim, based on the evidence you mentioned."

"When I receive the ballistics report, it should confirm the suspected weapon was a .38 caliber handgun. Once that's determined, I will check all the local and surrounding gun shops to see who may have bought a .38 caliber pistol in the last few years."

"What you're saying makes sense, Jim. However, that will be a big job, much bigger than one man can handle. I'll assign a couple of uniforms to do the work for you, and that will allow you to continue your investigation. Let me know when you receive the crime lab report, and we'll go from there."

"Thanks, Chief. I'm hoping to have it in a day or two."

As the chief's phone began ringing, Jim took that as his cue to exit.

Jim had no sooner sat at his desk when Craig Walker strolled into his office.

"Good morning, Jim. How's the murder investigation coming along?"

"Good morning, Craig. Things are in limbo until we receive the crime lab report."

"Good luck with the case. I'd better get moving. I just got called to a fender bender. See you later."

"Okay, see you, Craig."

A few seconds after Walker had left, Jim's phone rang.

"Detective Barkowsky."

"Good morning, Jim. It's Brad Strongman."

"Good morning, Brad." What the hell does he want now?

"I'm sorry to inform you, but I've been assigned to another case and will probably be tied up for a few weeks or more. My superiors don't have anyone else they can spare at this time. You're on your own until then, Jim." He laughed and said, "Try not to screw it up, okay!"

After hanging up, Jim smiled. Thank God! Maybe I can solve the case before Strongman comes back, the arrogant bastard.

Jim spent most of the day catching up on paperwork. It was six p.m., and his stomach began to rumble, reminding him that he hadn't eaten since breakfast.

As he was about to leave, Rusty Sykes appeared in the doorway.

"I hear you're investigating a homicide at the asshole's cabin. Do you have any leads so far?"

It's none of your fucking business. Trying to be civil, Jim replied, "Still too early to tell, and I should know more in a day or two. I'd love to stay and chat, Rusty, but I'm already late for dinner." With a wide grin, Jim said, "By the way, would you like me to say hello to Buck for you?"

Rusty's face turned beet-red, and he shot back, "You can tell that motherfucker to kiss my rosy red ass."

"Okay, Rusty, I'll pass those good wishes to Buck. Have a nice evening." Chuckling to himself, he grabbed his coat and left.

Shawna greeted Jim with a hug and a kiss as he entered the house.

"How was your day, honey?"

"Boring as hell. I met with the chief about the murder, cleaned up a ton of paperwork, and answered a few phone calls. The best news of the day was when Brad Strongman called to tell me he had to finish another case and won't be available to screw things up for a couple of weeks or more. I'm ready for a drink or three to celebrate the good news."

"You don't like Brad Strongman too much, do you?"

"I don't dislike many people, but he's at the top of my shit list, one notch below Rusty. He's always so damn condescending, and he thinks his shit doesn't stink. Enough about Brad Strongman. How was your day, sweetheart?"

"Since it's Monday, we weren't busy at the shop today. I Did a few shampoos and cuts. Nothing too exciting. Someone spilled the beans because everyone in town is talking about the murder. Brenda Sykes came in for a cut and asked me for the scoop on what happened at Buck's cabin. I played dumb, which wasn't hard to do," Shawa laughed.

Shawna owned a beauty salon on Mill Street. Several hairdressers worked for her, and she enjoyed running her own business. Her salon was ideal for catching up on all the local gossip.

Jim asked, "Where's Buck?"

"When he returned from the cabin, Buck said he wanted barbecue steaks for us tonight. He left about forty minutes ago to pick them up, along with a few other things he said he needed. He should be back soon."

Just then, they heard Buck's truck pull into the driveway. A few minutes later, smiling, he came through the front door juggling three grocery bags.

"Hey guys," Buck said cheerily, "I hope you're hungry."

Jim said, "Nice of you to cook dinner, my friend. I'm sure Shawna appreciates having a night off. Should I keep the heartburn medication handy?"

"Jim," Shawna scolded, "that's not nice! Buck, ignore him."

Jim gave a devilish grin and said, "Just kidding. We do appreciate it, Buck, old man."

"It's not much, but it's the least I can do to thank you guys for your hospitality."

Buck took out a bucket of vanilla ice cream and put it into the freezer. Then he removed five thick T-bone steaks, green beans, a bag of potatoes, lettuce, tomatoes, cucumbers, strawberries, and two bottles of an expensive French Merlot.

Buck opened a bottle of wine, poured two glasses, and handed one to Jim and Shawna. He smiled and said, "Go get lost in the family room while the chef creates his masterpiece."

As they were leaving, Buck went to work creating the salad. After completing that, he washed and prepared the beans and potatoes. Buck wrapped the green beans in tin foil with plenty of butter. Next, he wrapped each potato in tin foil, ready for baking. He marinated the steaks with a special sauce he had concocted, then went out to the deck and fired up the gas barbecue.

A few minutes later, Kristina and Nicolas burst through the front door, talking and giggling. They each grabbed a soda from the refrigerator and found their parents relaxing with a glass of wine in the family room.

Kristina asked, "Where's Uncle Buck?"

"Uncle Buck's out on the deck barbecuing our supper."

"Let's go say hello to the chef," Nicolas said.

They were still sitting around the dining room table an hour later, eating a bowl of ice cream topped with strawberries. Everyone congratulated Buck on the sumptuous dinner, and Buck said he was glad they had enjoyed the meal.

Nicolas and Kristina volunteered for cleanup duty and told the adults to relax in the family room.

After they had finished cleaning up, Kristina and Nicolas popped by to say goodnight.

"Anyone for a refill of wine?" Jim asked.

"I'll have another glass, please," Shawna said.

"Sounds good," Buck agreed.

Jim entered the kitchen, cracked the second bottle, poured three glasses, placed them on a tray, and returned to the family room.

When comfortable in his recliner, Jim looked at Buck with a silly grin and said, "You'll never guess who came into my office just as I was leaving."

"From the silly grin on your face, I'd have to say it was my old friend Rusty, 'Pothead,' Sykes."

"Bingo," Jim said. "I asked him if he wanted me to say hello to you, and he said, and I quote, 'Tell that motherfucker he can kiss my rosy red ass,' unquote."

Buck laughed so hard he almost choked on his wine.

"I didn't expect anything less from Rusty. I'm sure he's called me a lot worse than that over the years."

Shawna said, "You boys have never been able to get along, have you? You and Rusty have been feuding since middle school."

Buck chuckled. "It got worse in high school when Doreen dumped him for me."

Changing the subject, Jim said, "Did you return to the cabin today to check out the cleaning job?"

"I went to the cabin after lunch, and they were finishing up. The cleaning crew did an excellent job. The place looked nice and clean, but it still smelled of disinfectant. I stayed for a few hours and opened the doors and all the windows to let the place air out. Before leaving, I installed a new lock on the front door. I'm heading back tomorrow to make a list of all the things I need to fix. I'm planning on renovating the entire cabin. My priority is to hire a roofer to replace the shingles before we get too much rain. If I don't get that done soon, I'm sure the place will leak like a sieve."

They sat and talked until around ten. Shawna yawned, thanked Buck again for the great meal, excused herself, and headed to bed.

When the two men were alone, Jim poured a glass of whiskey for each of them and said, "Cheers."

"Cheers," Buck said. They raised their glasses and took a sip.

"Man, that Canadian whiskey's good," Buck said.

"None better," Jim replied. "What else did you do today?"

"I drove to the cemetery to visit my mom and grandparents' graves. I did a little weeding and left some flowers. I can't believe how long it's been since they all passed on. I said a few prayers and sat and reminisced about the good times. I could almost taste all those great home-cooked meals my mom and grandma used to make. I still have to smile when I think of fishing on Pushaw Lake. It seems like yesterday. When I was a kid, during summer vacation, grandpa used to take me out in his old wooden rowboat and teach me how to fish. Those were the days," Buck said with a broad smile. "After visiting the graves, I went to our old party spot on the river."

"Sounds like you were in a sentimental mood today," Jim said, smiling.

"I guess you could say that. It's the first time I've dared to revisit where Doreen vanished that night. I sat on a rock and did a lot of thinking. All the memories came flooding back. I relived that night over again. I even shed a few tears. Dammit, Jim, I still think what happened to Doreen wasn't an accident."

"You could be right, but how do we prove it?"

"I don't have a clue. What we need is a miracle," Buck said dejectedly. "Somehow, some way, I'm gonna get to the bottom of it."

CHAPTER 7

B lack clouds blocked the full moon. Doreen clawed at the water, screaming for help. Not a strong swimmer, the swift current began sweeping her away. Buck jumped in and swam as fast as he could toward her panicked screams. Briefly, he caught a glimpse of Doreen's terrified face. A second later, the swirling water pulled her under like a gigantic whale. Buck dove into the river, but the murky water prevented him from seeing a thing. He kept diving and coming up for air until he thought his lungs were about to burst. Suddenly, he saw Doreen reaching out to him, and he tried to grab her hand. For a brief moment, their fingertips touched. In a split second—Doreen had vanished.

Buck awoke in a panic. Sweat ran down his face like a river. He barely breathed and shook like a leaf in a violent windstorm. He could swear he had just completed a long-distance marathon. His thundering heart pounded inside his chest like it could explode any second. Gasping for air, it took him a few minutes to calm down. When he finally got his bearings, he realized he had just experienced another terrifying nightmare about Doreen.

Buck lay staring at the ceiling until daybreak. He was afraid to fall back to sleep for fear of another nightmare. He quietly slipped out of bed, got into his gray, fleece-lined track pants and matching top, pulled on a pair of socks, laced on his running shoes, and silently tiptoed down the stairs and out the front door, locking it behind him.

The morning air was fresh and cool, and it felt good to jog again. Since arriving back in Orono, he had neglected his exercise routine and thought he had packed on a few extra pounds from Shawna's great cooking and the booze he and Jim had been consuming.

As he left Perk O'Rock Landing Road, he turned left on Forest Avenue and headed for downtown. There wasn't a person or a car on the road this early. Buck had jogged for about thirty minutes, and he felt good—stress-free. As he began to cross Main Street, suddenly, a siren shrieked.

Out of nowhere, an Orono PD patrol car pulled up alongside him. The door opened, and out jumped Rusty Sykes.

What the fuck does he want?

"Good morning, asshole," Rusty said. "Tryin' to keep in shape, are you? Do you realize you just broke the law?"

"What the fuck are you talking about, Sykes?" Buck said, annoyed.

"You just jay-walked, or should I say, you just jay-ran?" Rusty said, laughing loudly. "Get it—jay-ran. I think I just created a new word." He began to laugh again. "Anyway, there's no traffic light here, so I'll have to write you up."

Rusty pulled out his book and began to write. When he finished, he handed Buck the ticket and said, "You can pay this at the police station. If it's not paid within five days, the fine will double, or you can take your chances in court. It's your choice, dickhead."

Buck looked at the ticket and saw it was for one hundred and fifty dollars. He threw it back at Rusty and said, "You can take your fucking ticket and shove it up your ass, Sykes."

Buck turned and slowly jogged away.

While all this was happening, Officer Sally White sat in the cruiser with an amused look.

Rusty bent down, picked up the ticket, ripped it into small pieces, threw them into the air, and watched as they blew away. Laughing, Rusty returned to the cruiser and, glancing at Sally, said, "Did you see the shocked look on his face? I think I got his blood pressure up a notch or two. Maybe the jerk will drop dead from a heart attack on his run. I can only hope."

Officer White stared straight ahead and didn't say a word.

When Buck returned from his run, he had a quick shower and joined everyone at the breakfast table. He decided to keep his run-in with Rusty to himself.

Shawna asked, "How did everyone sleep?"

Jim said, "I slept like a rock. I can't even remember dreaming."

Buck said, "I slept like a baby, and I felt so refreshed that I went for an early morning jog." The dark circles under his eyes told a different story.

Kristina and Nicolas both said they had slept well.

After Buck had left for the cabin and Kristina and Nicolas headed off to school, Shawna said, "Jim, I'm concerned about Buck. He doesn't appear to be sleeping much, and I suspect he could be having nightmares. Last night I heard him mumbling in his sleep. Do you think he could have PTSD?"

"I don't know what to think," Jim lied. He decided to respect Buck's wishes and not tell Shawna about their conversation.

"I researched Google the other day and couldn't believe what I found. It said most battle-fatigued soldiers who return home after witnessing the gruesome scenes of war develop symptoms of PTSD. The statistics shocked me. On average, twenty-two military personnel commit suicide in the U.S. every day. Can you believe that, twenty-two every day? I don't think those statistics include jobs like cops, firefighters, and other stressful occupations," Shawana said.

"God, if they're correct, those stats are unbelievable! All we can do is keep an eye on him. We shouldn't bring up the subject unless he approaches us first. Buck has a lot of pride, and I suspect he keeps many things bottled up. They say war is hell. I'm sure Buck has been to hell and back. And being a homicide detective in New York City isn't a picnic in Central Park."

Jim felt guilty not telling Shawna what he knew about Buck, but he had made a promise and was damn well going to keep it.

"Let's hope he doesn't do anything rash," Shawna said, looking concerned.

"I'm sure he'll be fine," Jim said.

As Buck drove, his mind started racing. His thoughts went back to the night of Doreen's death. For some reason, he couldn't shake the feeling that her drowning was not an accident.

Why had Rusty Sykes vanished from the party around the same

time as Doreen? Why was her necklace missing, and why didn't Rusty attend Doreen's funeral? Was this his way of getting even? Was he thinking, if I can't have her, neither can you, Buck Woods?

If Rusty did have anything to do with Doreen's death, how can I find proof after all these years?

As he pulled into the laneway, Buck made a mental note to talk to Jim about it again when the timing was right.

CHAPTER 8

It was a few minutes after ten the next morning when Jim received an email from the crime lab. He downloaded it and saved it to his document file. Jim printed a copy and began to read.

Dental records identified the victim. He was forty-seven-year-old Wayne Daniel Blackmore, a real estate broker and owner of All-Star Realty, Inc., in Bangor. DNA from the cigarette butts found in the kitchen, the blood on the bedroom floor, and the semen stains matched Blackmore.

The DNA from the blonde hairs on the pillow matched the DNA found on the two lipstick-stained cigarette filters. No records were on file to identify the mystery woman.

Fingerprints on the front door and lock matched the victim. A few others prints belonged to Buck. Before leaving, Doug Graham had taken Buck's fingerprints to eliminate them from other fingerprints.

The ballistics report confirmed the .38 caliber shell casing matched the slug. No gunshot residue (GSR) was on the victim's hands, eliminating any possibility of suicide.

The victim had died from a single gunshot wound to the head fired at close range. The estimated distance was six to ten feet.

Based on the state of decomposition of the body, the time of death was estimated to be seven to ten days before discovery.

The autopsy showed that Wayne Daniel Blackmore was a heavy smoker with early-stage lung cancer.

Dr. Corey Chambers included the phone number for Mrs. Donna Blackmore and asked Jim to call and break the sad news.

Jim preferred to deliver bad news in person, but there wasn't time for that. He picked up the phone and dialed the number.

The phone rang several times. Jim was about to hang up when a female voice answered.

"Hello."

"Is this Mrs. Blackmore?" Jim asked.

"Yes, I'm Donna Blackmore."

"Mrs. Blackmore, my name is Detective Jim Barkowsky with the Orono Police Department. I'm sorry, but I have bad news about your husband."

"I was expecting someone would be calling about Wayne. Was he in an accident? Is he hurt?"

"There's no easy way to say this, Mrs. Blackmore." Jim paused for a moment. "Your husband's body was discovered in a Pushaw Lake cabin near Orono. I'm sorry to have to tell you that he was murdered."

There was silence for a brief moment, and Jim heard gasping sobs as she broke down. He let her cry for a few minutes before asking, "Mrs. Blackmore, are you still there? Are you all right?"

A few seconds passed, and she finally said, between sobs, "Yes, Detective, I'm here. I'm okay." She doesn't sound okay. "I don't know how to tell my two boys about their father's death. They'll be devastated."

"How old are your boys, Mrs. Blackmore?"

"Billy is fifteen, and Bobby is seventeen."

"I'm so sorry, Mrs. Blackmore. I wish to extend my heartfelt condolences to you and your boys."

"Thank you, Detective."

Jim went on to tell her that her husband's body would be released to her chosen funeral home.

"When you know the name of the funeral home, I will call the medical examiner's office and inform them for you."

"I would appreciate that very much, Detective. Wayne prepaid his cremation. Please have his body sent to the Rest-in-Peace funeral home in Bangor."

"No problem, Mrs. Blackmore, I'll take care of it immediately.

Next, Jim told her about her husband's early-stage lung cancer.

Still sobbing, she asked, "If Wayne hadn't been shot, do you think he would have died from lung cancer?"

"Not being a doctor, that's not for me to say, Mrs. Blackmore."

Just before hanging up, Donna reluctantly agreed to meet him the following day for an interview.

Jim printed another copy of the report for Chief Durham. When the chief saw Jim, he waved him in.

"What's up, Jim?"

"I received the crime lab report a few minutes ago, Chief. Here's your copy."

Chief Durham took a few minutes to scan the report, then looked up and said, "Wayne Blackmore, huh? I know who he is, but I've never met him. Do you have any idea who the mystery woman might be?" As an afterthought, the chief said, "Lung cancer, eh? The poor bugger probably didn't even know he had it."

"I don't know who the woman could be, Chief, but that's what I intend to find out. If we can do that, the case could solve itself. I agree that Blackmore's cancer may have killed him before too long. However, with all the new drugs, you never know. He might have gotten several more years, or he could have lived a full life. One just never knows."

"As I mentioned the other day, Jim, I'm assigning two uniforms, Craig Walker and Mark Talbot, to canvass the gun shops. Talbot is on another assignment, but I'll make him available tomorrow morning. I'll assign Rusty to finish up what Mark was doing."

Jim was glad Rusty wasn't one of the officers assigned to the gun shop survey.

"Okay, Chief. Guess I'd better get things in motion."

After leaving the chief's office, Jim contacted Craig Walker and Mark Talbot and arranged to meet with them in his office at nine the following day. He told Mark the chief was reassigning him to work the case until further notice.

Jim searched the Internet for a list of gun shops in Maine, and his findings totaled ninety-three. He printed off a copy of the list and then highlighted all the shops within approximately a hundred-mile radius of Orono. It totaled sixty. He then made two lists of thirty and put them in the middle drawer of his desk. Jim prayed that the gun used in the murder had been purchased at one of the sixty shops.

Shawna was too tired to cook that evening, so they ordered pizza.

Later, Jim and Buck were alone, relaxing in the family room, nursing a couple of beers, when Buck said, "There's something I want to get your opinion on."

Jim nodded and said, "I'm all ears. Shoot."

"Last night, we discussed my suspicions that Doreen's death wasn't accidental. I suspect Rusty Sykes might have had something to do with it. It seems too much of a coincidence that Rusty vanished around the same time Doreen went missing. When they pulled her body from the river, Doreen's necklace wasn't around her neck. Rusty didn't attend Doreen's funeral, using the lame excuse that he was home in bed with the flu. He also said that he was going to get even with me. It all stinks like a tub of rotting fish. In my heart, I know that Rusty's hiding something."

Jim sighed and said, "What you're saying seems to make sense, but how do we prove it? The police interviewed everyone that night, including Rusty, and no one said they saw anything. Since there was no evidence of foul play, the police ruled Doreen's death an accident."

"That's the problem. Unless we can come up with an eyewitness who saw Rusty push Doreen into the river, we're screwed." Then Buck grinned and said, "The only other suggestion is to beat the shit out of him until he confesses."

Laughing, Jim said, "There's nothing I'd like better, but unfortunately, as you know, a confession obtained under duress wouldn't stand up in court. So, for now, you're right. We're screwed."

They decided there was nothing more they could accomplish that night. Buck got up, stretched, and headed for the stairs, and Jim did the same.

A half-hour later, while Buck was snoring and mumbling in his sleep, Jim tiptoed downstairs and downed a couple of shots of whiskey. At 4:10 a.m., he awoke in his recliner. Quietly, he went upstairs and slipped into bed, snuggling up to Shawna's warm body.

CHAPTER 9

The next morning, Buck was out the door by eight. He had hired a roofing company to reshingle the roof, and they were to start today. On the way, Buck stopped to pick up planks and support pillars for the front porch. By the time he arrived, the roofers were already hard at work.

At nine a.m., Craig Walker and Mark Talbot arrived at Jim's office. Neither of them looked pleased to be there.

After a brief greeting and small talk, Jim said it was time to get down to business. He pulled out the two lists from his middle drawer and gave each officer a copy. The lists contained the names, addresses, and telephone numbers of all the gun shops to be contacted.

"I want you to phone each gun shop and ask them to email you a list of all sales of .38 caliber pistols within the last five years. We'll need the purchase date, name of the purchaser, address, and phone number. Once you have that information, you'll have to phone each buyer to see if they still have the gun. Then all the pistols must be borrowed so the crime lab can do a ballistics analysis. I know this is a lot of work and a long shot, but if it solves Wayne Blackmore's murder, it will be well worth it."

Mark Talbot laughed and said, "Long shot or not, it'll give me a break from pounding the beat."

Craig Walker agreed. "Let's get right to it. The sooner we start, the sooner we'll be done."

"That's the attitude, guys. If there's nothing else, then let's get at it. I'll be away for a few hours, and we can chat later."

"Where will you be if we need to get a hold of you?" Craig Walker asked.

"I'll be in Bangor interviewing the widow of the murder victim. You can reach me on my cell, but if you have to call, be damned sure it's important."

Jim arrived in Bangor shortly after ten-thirty. His appointment with Donna Blackmore was scheduled for eleven. They were to meet at the Tim Hortons coffee shop just off I-95 at exit 1A across the highway from the Bangor Municipal Golf Course. Jim purchased a large black coffee, found a table in a quiet corner, and sat down to wait.

Shortly after eleven, a striking woman in her mid-forties with curves in all the right places walked through the door. She wore a Boston Red Sox baseball cap, and dark sunglasses covered her eyes. A shoulder-length auburn ponytail hung out the opening of the hat. Her navy blue knit sweater contrasted with her skin-tight faded blue jeans and white jogging shoes.

Wow! Donna Blackmore is a sexy woman. Why would her husband cheat on her?

Over his years as a police officer, Jim had learned one valuable lesson—never pre-judge anything until you have all the facts.

Looking around, she spotted Jim and gracefully moved in his direction. He had given her his description yesterday when he had called to break the bad news of her husband's death.

She raised her pencil-thin eyebrows, smiled, and said, "You must be Detective Barkowsky."

Jim stood, returned her smile, extended his hand, and said, "I'm pleased to meet you, Mrs. Blackmore. I only wish it was under happier circumstances. Once again, you have my deepest sympathy and condolences."

"Thank you, Detective," she said.

After she took a seat, Jim asked, "Would you care for a coffee and a doughnut or something?"

She laughed. "Doughnuts don't agree with my waistline, but I would love a medium black coffee without sugar, please, if it's not too much trouble."

"No trouble at all." Jim left and returned in a few minutes with her coffee.

As he sat down, the captivating citrus fragrance from her delightful perfume drifted into his nostrils.

"I'd like to thank you, Mrs. Blackmore, for agreeing to meet me on such short notice. I know how hard this must be for you, but the sooner we can piece things together, the quicker we'll be able to catch and bring your husband's killer to justice."

"Please, Detective, call me Donna."

"Okay then, Donna, please start from the last time you saw your husband alive."

She paused and removed her sunglasses, revealing bloodshot blue eyes. She gazed directly at Jim and said, "To be honest, Wayne and I were having marital problems. We'd been arguing a lot lately, and I suspected he was going through a mid-life crisis. He was spending more time out of town on business trips, which I found unusual. When he left on March 30th, Wayne told me he needed time to think. He said he had rented a cabin on a lake and would be gone for about ten days. Wayne planned to read, relax and escape the rat race. He told me the cabin was in a remote part of the state and that no landline or cell phone service was available. That's when I suspected he might be having an affair. I had no proof, so I didn't want to jump to conclusions. I began to worry when he failed to return home after twelve days. On day thirteen, yesterday, I was about to contact the police when you called to break the horrible news. My two sons have been devastated by their father's death. I think I will end up a basket case before this is all over."

Jim could see tears forming in her swollen blue eyes, and her hands began to tremble.

"I can't even begin to imagine what you must be going through. I only have a few more questions, if that's okay?"

She sniffled, took a tissue from her purse, dabbed at her eyes, then said, "Go ahead, Detective."

"You said your husband left on the 30th of April. Can you tell me what kind of car he was driving?"

"Yes, Wayne drives, or should I say drove, a black Cadillac. I believe it's called an SRX Crossover. Why do you ask?"

"When his body was found, your husband's watch, ring, and identification were missing, and his car was not at the crime scene. The crime lab identified him through dental records. Was your husband's watch expensive, and did he usually carry a lot of cash?"

"Wayne's watch was a Rolex. As for cash, I'm not sure. Wayne usually charged most purchases to credit cards, especially business expenses. Are you saying he was robbed when he was murdered, and the killer took his car?"

"That could be one possibility, or the killer may want us to think that. I'm not ruling anything out at this point."

Donna Blackmore began to sob once more. She fumbled in her purse, took out another tissue, wiped her eyes, blew her nose, licked her pouty pink lips, took a long, deep breath, and composed herself. After another short pause, she said, "Sorry, Detective, I'm having difficulty controlling my emotions."

"That's quite all right, Donna. Take your time. There's no rush."

When he sensed she was ready to continue, Jim asked, "Can you think of anyone who would want to harm your husband—any threats or enemies you know of?"

She hesitated for a long moment as if considering the question, then said, "I can't think of anyone who would want to harm him. Wayne was well-liked. His friends and staff all thought the world of him. He was always fair and generous regarding his sales and secretarial staff—bonuses at Christmas, that sort of thing."

"Do you own a .38 caliber handgun?"

The question caught Donna off guard. Anger flashed in her eyes, and she raised her voice. "I can't believe it! You think I killed my husband?"

A few people began to stare in their direction.

Jim said calmly, "I'm not saying that. I wouldn't be doing my job if I didn't ask."

Lowering her voice, Donna said, "Well, for your information, Mr. Detective, I do own a pistol, and I keep it in the house in case of a break-in. Wayne insisted I have a gun for protection; he even made me take lessons to learn how to shoot. If I remember correctly, it's a .22 caliber Smith & Wesson."

"Do you know if your husband owned a .38 caliber handgun?"

"I think he owned a gun, but I don't know much about it. I believe he might have kept it in the glove compartment of his car."

"Did Wayne owe large sums of money to anyone, such as a gambling debt?"

"No, to the best of my knowledge, Wayne never gambled. He bought and sold real estate occasionally, but that was his business. I don't consider that to be gambling."

"Thank you, Donna, for meeting with me today." He handed her his card, making direct eye contact. "If you think of anything that might help our investigation, please call me anytime. I hope you don't mind, but I may need to talk with you again soon."

"Sorry for getting angry, Detective. I understand you're doing your job and must check out all possible suspects. I guess I'm a little stressed out. No hard feelings?"

"No hard feelings. I'll do my best to keep you updated on our investigation."

They shook hands, said goodbye, and left the coffee shop.

On his drive home, Jim kept reviewing the interview in his mind. He thought. Donna Blackmore seemed legitimately distraught. Based on what she told me, I can eliminate her as a suspect for now.

When he arrived at his office, Jim went online and obtained the plate number for Wayne Blackmore's Cadillac. After receiving the information, he put out a BOLO to all police departments in Maine, hoping that someone would find the vehicle.

Next, he checked his voicemail, and there was a message to call Mr. Frank Zubba, Manager, Global World Insurance, Inc., in Bangor, on his direct line.

Jim dialed the number, and after the fourth ring, a husky voice said, "Good afternoon, Frank Zubba."

Jim said, "Good afternoon Mr. Zubba. It's Detective Barkowsky from the Orono PD returning your call."

"Thanks for getting back to me, Detective. I understand that you're the detective handling the Wayne Blackmore murder investigation. Is that correct?"

"Yes, I'm one of them," Jim replied.

"I called to inform you that our company holds an insurance policy for two million dollars on Mr. Blackmore's life. The beneficiary of the policy is Donna Joan Blackmore. The policy is not payable if the death was a suicide. Has that possibility been ruled out?"

"Yes, the death has been ruled a homicide. Should you require one, the Rest-in-Peace funeral home in Bangor will have a death certificate on file."

"Do you have any suspects?"

"We are in the early stages of our investigation, and there's nothing more I can disclose now."

"Okay, thanks, Detective. I appreciate the information," Frank Zubba said.

After the call ended, Jim thought. The insurance policy has cast an entirely different light on things. Donna Blackmore had two million reasons to want her husband dead. If she didn't pull the trigger, she would have more than enough money to hire someone to do the job for her. The shot to the middle of the forehead looks like a Mafia-style hit. Donna seemed so distraught during the interview. Was she sincere, or was she playacting? Donna Blackmore is now my number one suspect.

Since Jim had returned from Bangor earlier than expected, he checked with Craig and Mark, and they were still busy making phone calls. They agreed to meet in Jim's office at nine in the morning to update him.

Jim stopped by Chief Durham's office and gave him a synopsis of his conversations with Donna Blackmore and Frank Zubba.

After Jim finished, the chief said, "I think we'd better try to find out more about Donna Blackmore. She has a few reasons to want her husband dead—his infidelity and the life insurance money. She goes to the top of the list until we develop more suspects. If we can find the murder weapon, it would certainly help. Keep digging, Jim."

Jim left the meeting with Chief Durham feeling a little down and frustrated. Unless the gun shop search discovers the owner of the murder weapon, it's going to be challenging to find the killer. The killer would have to be crazy to have kept the gun, and anyone in his right mind would have gotten rid of it. If I can find Wayne Blackmore's lover, the mystery woman, she could be the killer or know who shot Wayne Blackmore.

At that moment, a light went on. Jim had a plan!

CHAPTER 10

O n his way home from the cabin, Buck decided to go to the Home Depot outlet in Bangor. He wanted to look for kitchen cabinets and appliances.

While browsing through a cabinet display, he felt a gentle tap on his shoulder, and a meek voice said, "Can I help you, sir?" Turning around, Buck saw a clerk in a Home Depot smock with a gap-toothed smile. The face looked familiar.

"I thought it was you, Buck," the familiar face said.

Buck was racking his brain, trying to find the name that matched his face. The man was three inches shorter than Buck and wore dark-framed horn-rimmed glasses. Then it dawned on him!

"Is that you, Terry?"

"It sure is, Buck. It's been a long time."

Buck was speaking with Terry Wells, the nerdy kid he had known from his middle school days—the kid Rusty Sykes took pleasure in bullying and the kid Buck tried to protect. When he was younger, Terry reminded him of the blond boy in the movie A Christmas Story, the kid with the horn-rimmed glasses that received a Red Ryder BB gun for Christmas.

"God, Terry, I almost didn't recognize you. I still picture you the way you looked back in our high school days. If I remember correctly, you were at the high school summer vacation party on the river the last time I saw you. Man, it seems like eons ago."

"Yeah, it's close to thirty years. It was a sad night because of what happened to your girlfriend, Doreen Warren. I know how distressed you and her parents were at the time. I'll never forget that tragic night. I'm so sorry, Buck."

"Thanks, Terry. I appreciate your concern. I'm curious, did you see our old nemesis, Rusty Sykes, that night?"

"Oh, yeah, but I tried to stay clear of him as much as possible. He was pretty high on pot."

"By any chance, did you see Rusty talking to Doreen that night?"

Terry hesitated, then said, "No, I didn't see them talking, but he may have followed her. I didn't think anything of it at the time. Rusty looked wasted and could barely walk, let alone follow anybody."

"After you heard Doreen had gone missing and was found dead the next day, did any alarm bells go off?"

"No. When the police had ruled Doreen's death an accident, I assumed they were right."

"Did you ever tell the police that you thought Rusty might have followed Doreen before she disappeared?"

"No, because I didn't know he followed her, and I didn't see anything. You know Rusty, he would have beaten the living crap out of me if he thought I was accusing him of something."

Buck said, more to himself than to Terry, "I guess we'll never know what happened that night. I still think Rusty had something to do with it, but suspecting and proving it after all these years will probably be impossible."

"By the way, Buck, what are you doing back in this neck of the woods? Pardon the pun."

Buck laughed and told Terry he was on vacation from the NYPD and about inheriting his grandfather's property. He mentioned staying with Jim and Shawna while renovating his cabin.

"I'm looking for kitchen cabinets, appliances, and bathroom fixtures."

"You've come to the right place, Buck. I'll be glad to help you find everything you need."

On his way home, Buck decided to stop for a beer at Kelly's.

After his encounter with Terry Wells, Buck felt mentally drained. He plopped himself down at the bar and ordered a Bud Light. He was thirsty, and the cold beer tasted good.

Buck was still thinking about his conversation with Terry when someone tapped him on his shoulder. A gravelly voice asked, "Is that you, Buck?"

Buck turned and saw another familiar face. This time the man was much older, and the wrinkles on his skin looked like a road map, but his eyes still had the same friendly twinkle that Buck remembered when he was much younger. His gray hair had thinned considerably since the last time Buck had seen him. He was staring at the face of former Police Chief Harold Barker, a close friend of his deceased grandfather, Bill Woods.

Breaking into a broad smile, Buck said, "Chief Barker, it's so nice to see you again. It's been a long time. Please join me, and let me buy you a drink?"

"Thanks, Buck, don't mind if I do. A beer would be good."

"What brand would you like, Chief?"

"I usually drink Miller Lite."

When his beer arrived, Buck said, "Cheers, Chief."

"Cheers, Buck." The chief raised his hand, and they clinked bottles.

After they both had taken a sip, the chief said, "The last time I remember seeing you was at your grandfather's funeral. As I recall, we talked briefly, and I haven't seen you since that day. Before that, it was way back when I was still in office when your girlfriend drowned. That was such a tragic time."

"Yes, it was, Chief. I know the police ruled her death an accident, but I've always had doubts."

"Oh, what makes you say that, Buck?"

"I don't have any proof, but I find it hard to believe that Doreen would trip and fall into the river. She wasn't a good swimmer, and she was always cautious around water."

"Well, Buck, all I can say is that we investigated thoroughly and interviewed all the kids, and no one could shed any light on what happened. Of course, maybe someone wasn't telling the truth, but there was no way we could prove it wasn't an accident. Just like you, I've always had my doubts as well."

"What about Rusty Sykes? Do you remember interviewing him?"

"I didn't interview any of the kids myself. The investigating officers did the interviewing, but I never liked Rusty. He was always a bit of a smart-ass. I suspected him of dealing pot, but we could never catch him in the act. Now I see he's on the Orono police force. I don't know how that happened. Guess he pulled the wool over someone's eyes," the chief said as he took another swig of his beer.

"You look to be in good shape, Chief. I hope you don't mind me asking, but how old are you?"

"I turned eighty a few months ago. I have type-two diabetes but I keep it in check with four metformin pills daily, diet, and exercise. I walk every day. I got this new device," he showed Buck the black band on his wrist, "it's called a Fitbit. Daily, it tracks how many steps I walk, my heart rate, the number of stairs I climb, the hours of sleep I get each night, and a few other things. I get a weekly report on my computer. They post different badges to your computer when you attain certain levels. It keeps me motivated. I got several badges, and my Japan badge was the most recent. They said I walked across Japan—1,869 miles. My goal is to walk a minimum of ten thousand steps every day. I try to do more than that. Most days, I walk six or seven miles. I bought it about a year ago, just after Edna passed away. It gets me out of the house, so I don't sit around feeling sorry for myself."

"It's great to hear you're staying in shape, Chief. Maybe I should get one of those devices. Sorry, I didn't hear of Edna's passing. You have my heartfelt condolences, Chief. She was a lovely woman, and everyone who knew her thought the world of Edna."

"She had a massive heart attack and died sitting in her recliner watching her favorite soap opera."

"I'm sure you miss her a lot."

"Yes, I do. I miss Edna's smile and her crazy sense of humor. It's been a hard year, but life must go on. I visit her grave every week, and we have a little chat. By the way, what brings you back to Orono?"

"I'm on vacation from the NYPD, and I returned to relax and renovate the cabin I inherited from my grandpa when he passed on."

"Good luck. I think you're gonna have your work cut out for you.

Before your grandfather died, I went to see him a few times. After your grandmother died, he didn't do much of anything and spent no time maintaining the cabin."

"You're right about that, Chief. If nothing else, it'll give me something to keep me occupied for a while." Glancing at his watch, Buck said, "Sorry, Chief, I've got to run. I don't want to be late for dinner. I'm staying with the Barkowsky family while I work on the cabin."

"Sounds like you plan on staying around a while. I heard the body of some real estate guy from Bangor was found in your cabin. Is that right?"?"

"Yeah, that's where Jim Barkowsky and I found him. Jim and Brad Strongman from the Maine State Police are working the case."

"Strongman, huh? Not one of my favorite people. Anyway, I hope they catch the killer. We usually don't have many murders around here. Well, Buck, I hope you enjoy your vacation. Give my regards to Jim and Shawna."

"Thanks, Chief. I'll say hello to them for you. Again, I'm so sorry to hear of Edna's passing."

As the chief drained his beer, he checked his Fitbit, laughed, and said, "Well, I guess I'd better get moving before I get rigor mortis. I need another thousand steps to meet my daily goal."

Later that evening, when Buck and Jim had a nightcap, Buck told the story of his conversation with Terry Wells and his encounter with former Chief Harold Barker.

"Wow," Jim said, "Terry's story seems to corroborate your thinking about Rusty. Too bad he didn't witness anything. We need hard evidence, something that will lead us to the truth."

"To change the subject, one other thing has been bothering me. When I was at the cabin today, I kept thinking about the crime scene and why the victim's vehicle was missing. Then it dawned on me. It could be in the lake, along with the murder weapon. The water at the end of the boat ramp drops off quickly, and I bet it's ten to twelve feet deep. Maybe you should call in a dive team to check it out. What do you think?"

"That's a hell of a good idea, Buck. I don't know why I didn't think of it. Guess I've been so involved with all the other details that I couldn't see the forest for the trees."

Buck laughed. "You can't think of everything, Telly. That's why I'm here. Two heads are better than one."

CHAPTER 11

Jim met with Mark and Craig the next morning to discuss their progress with the gun shops.

Sitting in Jim's office, Craig said, "We're almost done. It will probably take a few more days before the sales records arrive by email."

"Okay, keep on it," Jim said. "Once you get the results, the next step will be to contact the gun owners to verify possession. Then I want you to go to each owner and pick up the pistols. Issue a receipt, and tag each gun with every owner's name and contact information. When all the available guns have been collected, one of you will deliver them to the crime lab for ballistics testing."

Mark asked, "What if some of the owners aren't local, say, out of state, for instance?"

"Let's wait and see. Don't worry about it now. We'll deal with things as they come up."

The meeting ended, and everyone went back to work.

Jim couldn't stop thinking about the mystery woman. Yesterday, he called the office manager, Carl Parker of All-Star Realty, Inc., and asked him to set up a meeting with all employees. Mr. Parker later confirmed that the meeting had been scheduled for two today.

Jim went to see Chief Durham. He told him about Buck's idea to search the lake near the cabin for the murder weapon and Wayne Blackmore's vehicle. After listening closely, the chief said, "Jim, it certainly can't hurt. I'll call the Maine State Police and make the arrangements. As soon as I know the date, I'll let you know. You and Buck might want to be there."

Jim spent the rest of the morning catching up on paperwork. At noon, he met Shawna for a quick lunch at Woodman's Bar & Grill, then took off for Bangor.

It was one-thirty when Jim arrived at the All-Star Realty, Inc. building. He introduced himself to the receptionist, whose desk plaque showed the name Janis Cromwell. Janis was in her mid to late thirties, attractive and petite, with long red hair, dark blue eyes, and milky-white skin.

Janis smiled warmly and said, "Mr. Parker is expecting you, Detective. Please follow me."

As Jim was ushered into his office, Carl Parker rose from his chair, smiled, extended his hand, and said, "It's a pleasure to meet you in person, Detective."

While shaking hands, Jim said, "Nice to meet you, Carl."

He sat down in one of the two brown leather armchairs.

Carl Parker, in his mid-thirties, sat behind a light oak desk, and his body more than filled the brown leather executive chair. His overweight mid-section hung over his belt. Almost completely bald, Parker had a terrible comb-over with the few strands of black hair he had left. His face was round and plump, with smooth skin, and his eyes reminded Jim of a sad hound dog.

A business degree from Boston University hung on the wall behind him. Two beige file cabinets stood against the back wall to his right.

"Can I offer you a coffee, Detective?"

"That would be great."

"Would you like cream and sugar?"

"No, thanks. Black will do just fine."

Parker punched the intercom button and said. "Janis, please bring us two black coffees, no sugar."

Ten minutes after delivering their coffee, the two men were making small about the Red Sox when Janis returned and said, "Carl, everyone's assembled in the meeting room—if you're ready."

"Thanks, Janis. Well, Detective, it looks like it's time to get the show on the road."

Jim followed Carl Parker down the hallway and turned left into a large room with approximately twenty people engrossed in conversation.

As Parker stepped to the podium, the talking abruptly ceased, and a hush fell over the room.

"May I have your attention, please? You all know why we're here today. At this time, I would like to introduce Detective Jim Barkowsky of the Orono Police Department."

Jim took Carl Parker's place at the podium. "Thank you, Mr. Parker. Good afternoon, ladies and gentlemen. As you may already know, I'm one of the detectives assigned to investigate the death of the owner of All-Star Realty, Inc., Mr. Wayne Blackmore. I want to express my sympathy for losing your boss and friend. Our job is to find his killer and bring them to justice, and I hope you can help me accomplish that today."

Jim gave some general details of the crime, then said, "We suspect that Mr. Blackmore was having a relationship with an unidentified blonde woman. We have been trying to locate this person but so far have been unsuccessful. If any of you have seen Mr. Blackmore with a blonde woman over the past few months, we would appreciate you coming forward."

Just as Jim finished, an attractive young woman held up her hand.

"Yes," Jim said.

"I'm Patty Johnson, a sales rep here at All-Star. In late January, we had a seminar in Bangor. The seminar, 'Spring into Spring,' was attended by local agents and agents from other towns and cities in Maine. Wayne was one of the guest speakers. After his speech, I saw him speaking with a pretty, middle-aged blonde woman. They appeared to be very friendly with one another. Later, I saw them chatting in a coffee shop down the street."

"Did you recognize the woman?"

"I've never seen her before. I don't think she was from Bangor."

Just then, a few more hands shot up, and several others said they had also seen them together.

"Would you be able to identify this woman if you saw her again?"

"Yes," Patty said, "I'm sure I would."

A few others said they were sure they could identify her as well.

Good, now we're getting somewhere.

Before leaving, Jim stopped by Carl Parker's office. "Carl, can I ask you to do me a big favor?"

"Sure, Detective. What can I do for you?"

"I was hoping you could get me a list of all the females who attended the conference. It would help if you could get me their pictures as well."

"That shouldn't be a problem. The Bangor Real Estate Board organized and sponsored the seminar. They will have a list of all the agents who attended, plus all the real estate offices will have pictures of all their sales reps. I should be able to have everything for you in a day or two. I'll get Janis on it immediately. I'll call you as soon as I have the information."

"Thanks, Carl. I appreciate your help. When you get the pictures, we can have Patty look at them to see if she can find the woman we're looking for."

"No problem, Detective. Talk to you soon."

As Jim walked out the front door of the All-Star Realty building, several reporters, including a TV crew, surrounded him.

How did they know I'd be here? Someone must have spilled the beans.

Sharon Cox, an aggressive news reporter from a local TV station, stuck a microphone in front of his face and asked, "Detective Barkowsky do you have any suspects in the Wayne Blackmore homicide?"

"Yeah, what's going on, Detective?" another reporter asked.

"Sorry folks, we're in the early stage of our investigation, and I have nothing to say."

"Come on, Detective, you've got to give us something," another reporter yelled.

Jim pushed his way past the reporters and trotted to his car. They ran after him like a pack of hounds hot on the scent of a fox.

On the drive to Orono, Jim was feeling optimistic. *Will I soon know the identity of the mystery woman?*

CHAPTER 12

The next morning, Jim was sitting at his desk pondering how close he was getting to identifying the mystery woman when Chief Durham called him into his office.

"Jim, I just received a call from the Maine State Police, and they're sending a dive team to Buck's cabin this afternoon at two. You and Buck should be there."

"Okay, Chief, I'll call Buck."

Jim arrived at the cabin at one-forty-five and found Buck sitting on the newly renovated front porch sipping a beer.

"Hey, B.J.," Jim said. "You look relaxed."

Buck laughed and said, "I'm on a union break, and I thought I'd have a beer while I waited for you. It was good of Chief Durham to call in the Maine State Police dive team. You never know what they'll find."

"It's worth a shot. We might get lucky."

A few minutes later, the sound of a motor and tires crunching gravel echoed from the far end of the laneway. In seconds, an aqua-colored SUV of the Maine State Police Underwater Recovery Team pulled in next to Jim's car. The vehicle trailered a small aluminum boat with a 15-horsepower Mercury outboard motor.

Three men exited the vehicle and walked toward Jim and Buck, who came to greet them.

A good-looking, muscular man in his mid-thirties with short, dark hair extended his hand toward Jim and said, "Detective Jim Barkowsky, it's good to see you again."

"It's great to see you as well, Grant. It's been a few years. I'd like you to meet my friend and owner of the property, Buck Woods. Buck is on vacation from his job as a homicide detective with the NYPD. Buck, this is Team Commander Grant Mathews."

They shook hands, and Grant said, "It's a pleasure to meet you, Buck. Hope your vacation is going well."

Buck laughed and replied, "It was until we found a dead body in my cabin."

"Yeah, that's not the best way to start a vacation. Hopefully, it will only get better from here."

"I hope so," Buck laughed. "I'm used to seeing dead bodies, but finding a corpse inside my cabin was a little upsetting and an unpleasant surprise."

"As you were no doubt informed, we're looking for the victim's missing vehicle and the possible murder weapon, which we suspect could be in the lake," Jim said.

"That's why we're here," Nodding at the two younger men, Grant said, "These are my teammates, Greg Thomas and Justin Gordon." They shook hands with Jim and Buck.

After a few minutes of small talk, Grant returned to the SUV, backed it down the concrete ramp, and slid the boat off the trailer into the water. The team changed into their dive skins, ready to go. Before leaving, they threw underwater lights and flippers into the boat. Once everyone was on board, Grant started the motor, and the boat slowly moved away. They circled a few times, and a short distance in front of the boat ramp, the motor stopped, and Justin lowered the anchor. Jim and Buck watched as the three divers, holding their dive lights, disappeared beneath the surface.

"There's nothing we can do here," Buck said. "Let's return to the cabin, and I'll buy you a beer."

"Okay, I'm not returning to the station, so one beer can't hurt."

Twenty minutes later, Buck and Jim decided to see how the drivers were doing. They were staring at an empty boat when suddenly, an orange marker bobbed to the surface.

Pointing at the marker, Buck said, "Hey, did you see that?"

"Yeah, partner, it looks like they must've found something and are marking the spot."

"I bet they found Blackmore's vehicle," Buck said.

In a few minutes, the divers surfaced and climbed back into the boat, and Greg pulled the anchor while Grant started the motor. When they reached shore, Jim could hardly contain himself.

Excited, Jim asked, "Hey, Grant, what did you find?"

Smiling, Grant said, "It looks like it's the victim's vehicle you've been searching for."

"I knew it," Buck said. "The killer or killers must have pushed or driven it into the lake after the murder."

"Did you have any luck finding a gun?" Jim asked.

Grant pulled a water-soaked pistol from his waist pouch and said, "I found it in the glove box."

"Holy shit, you guys are amazing," Buck said.

The pistol turned out to be a compact .38 caliber Glock Model 42.

"We'd better get this gun to the crime lab," Jim said. "Let's hope it's the murder weapon. Why would the killer put it back into the glove box if Blackmore's gun is the murder weapon.? That doesn't make sense. I would've tossed into the lake."

"I guess we'll just have to wait and see if it matches," Buck said.

Jim went to his car and came back with an evidence bag. Wearing latex gloves, he dropped the pistol into the plastic bag, sealed it, and filled out and signed the label.

"Well, that's all we can do today," Grant said. "I'll arrange for the Maine State Police to pull the vehicle out of the lake, and we'll come back to hook it up at that time. Someone will call with a date and time, Jim."

"Okay, thanks, Grant," Jim said.

After loading the boat onto the trailer, the three divers changed out of their scuba gear, got into the SUV, said goodbye, and left.

Jim and Buck stood staring at the lake for several seconds.

Finally, Buck found his tongue and said, "That was quite the afternoon."

"Yeah, it sure was. Let's head back to the house and call it a day. I'll have the gun sent over to the crime lab first thing in the morning."

"Sounds good to me," Buck said. "We can have a drink or two and celebrate finding another piece of the puzzle."

CHAPTER 13

The next morning, sitting in Chief Durham's office, Jim updated him on the dive team's discovery. When Jim finished, the chief said, "Finding the car solves one part of the mystery, and finding Wayne Blackmore's gun might solve another part of the puzzle. I'll have an officer drive the gun to the crime lab today for ballistics testing. Hopefully, we should know in a day or two if it's the murder weapon."

"It'll be interesting to see what they find. Grant Mathews said the gun was in the glove box, where Donna Blackmore thought her husband might have kept it. If the killer used Wayne Blackmore's gun to murder him, why would they put it back into the glove box? It doesn't seem logical to me."

"You're right. It doesn't seem logical. Who knows what killers think? People do strange things when they're under pressure."

"Since Wayne Blackmore's car was in the lake, I don't think one person put it there. I suspect it would take a couple of people to push it down the ramp and into the water."

"Good point, Jim." Unless," the chief smiled, "that person was as strong as The Hulk."

After meeting with the chief, his phone rang when Jim returned to his desk.

"Detective, Barkowsky."

"Good morning, Detective. It's Carl Parker."

"Good morning, Carl. What's up?"

"I've just received the pictures and names of all the females who attended the seminar. As it turned out, the Bangor Real Estate Board had the list, and all the pictures were also in their computer system."

"That's great news," Jim said. "When can I drop by to check them out?"

"Would two this afternoon work for you, Detective? If it does, I'll have Patty Johnson here to view the photos to see if she can find the woman you're looking for."

"Two will be fine. I'll see you then."

As Jim hung up, a broad smile lit up his face. *Now we're getting somewhere!*

Jim arrived at the All-Star Realty reception desk shortly before two o'clock. Janis Cromwell greeted him with a friendly smile and told Jim that Carl Parker and Patty Johnson were waiting for him in Carl's office.

Jim took a deep breath, crossed his fingers, and started down the hallway. Patty was drinking coffee and chatting with Carl as he entered the office. After exchanging pleasantries, Carl handed Jim the list of all female seminar attendees and lined up ten pictures on his desk for Patty to view. Just then, Janis entered with two cups of black coffee, handed one to Jim and Carl, and left.

Before Jim could read the names on the list, Patty began to look at the pictures. She stopped, studied one closely, and held it up. "This is her, the woman I saw with Wayne." She smiled, waving the picture in the air.

When Jim looked at the photograph, he could hardly believe his eyes. The mystery woman was Brenda Sykes. Scanning the list, he found her name.

Jim asked, "Patty, are you positive this is the woman you saw talking with Wayne Blackmore, the one at the seminar and in the coffee shop?"

"Yes, Detective, I'm positive."

Wow! Rusty's wife. He would never have guessed. Jim saw Brenda occasionally at social functions and the odd time with Rusty at Kelly's—like the other night during Rusty's confrontation with Buck. Brenda was the highest-producing sales representative at Big River Real Estate in Orono.

"Patty, Carl, I'd like to thank you for your time and help. Now that we know who the mystery woman is, it could go a long way in helping us solve Wayne Blackmore's murder."

As he exited the building this time, there wasn't a reporter in sight. Strolling toward his car, Jim whistled a happy tune, but his mind was zooming a mile a minute as questions popped into his head. Why was Brenda cheating on Rusty? Were they having marital problems? Did Rusty know about his wife's involvement with Wayne Blackmore? Did Brenda kill Wayne Blackmore? Did Rusty kill Wayne Blackmore? Did Rusty or Brenda own a .38 caliber pistol? Will the DNA from the blonde hairs and cigarette butts at the crime scene match Brenda?

Sooner or later, these questions would need to be answered. Since Rusty was a member of the Orono Police Department, things were much more complicated.

When Jim returned to the station, he headed straight into Captain Tony Timpano's office.

Short and stocky, Captain Tony Timpano was in his mid-fifties. He had broad shoulders, a square jaw, and deep-set brown eyes. His straight black hair showed gray at the temples, and his face looked tanned, having just returned from a week's golfing vacation in Florida. Captain Timpano, a veteran of twenty-four years on the Orono PD, was next in command under Chief Durham.

Jim rapped on his door, and Timpano waved him in.

"Hi, Jim, what's up?"

Jim gave him a brief update on the Blackmore case and asked the captain to accompany him to Chief Durham's office.

Seeing the two men approach, the chief motioned for them to enter. When they were seated, he asked, "What's going on, gentlemen?"

Jim said, "Chief, we finally caught a break in the Wayne Blackmore case. I'm glad you're sitting down because you won't believe this. The mystery woman has been identified as Brenda Sykes."

At first, the chief looked stunned, then composed himself and asked, "Are you sure, Jim?"

"Yes, Chief, she was identified from a picture as the woman seen talking with Wayne Blackmore at the seminar and in a coffee shop. Brenda Sykes attended a real estate seminar in Bangor this past January. I have a list of all attendees, and her name is on it."

"Since Rusty is a member of the force, this could be a delicate situation, Chief," Captain Timpano said.

"I agree, Captain. How are you planning on handling it, Jim?"

"The first thing we'll need to do is to get a DNA sample from Brenda Sykes. If her DNA matches the DNA found at the crime scene, we'll know she's the woman we've been searching for. The next step is determining if she or Rusty owns a .38 caliber pistol. This information could turn up in the gun shop search that Craig and Mark are doing. If Rusty had anything to do with the murder or suspects his wife is the killer, he may try to hide this information to protect her."

"Can I make a suggestion?" Captain Timpano asked.

"By all means," the chief said.

"Jim should approach Brenda Sykes on the QT without involving Rusty. Inform her of our findings and ask her to undergo a DNA test. It doesn't make sense to proceed with the gun question unless we get a positive match on the DNA. If the DNA doesn't match, there's no way we can place her at the crime scene. Therefore, the gun question would be irrelevant."

"Good thinking, Captain. Jim, let's proceed in that direction."

"Okay, Chief, I'll start working on it."

"By the way, Jim, since we're a little short-staffed and operating on a tight budget, Captain Timpano has volunteered to help with the investigation."

"Let me know if you need me to do anything, Jim," Tony said.

"Okay. Thanks, Captain."

After the meeting, Jim returned to his office and called Big River Real Estate. When Brenda Sykes came on the line, Jim said, "Hi, Brenda, Jim Barkowsky, here. I've got something important I'd like to discuss with you, and I would prefer to do it in person. Can you meet me for a coffee at the Verve in about a half hour?"

Brenda agreed without asking why.

When Brenda arrived, Jim was waiting in a lounge chair on the upper level, away from the crowd. Brenda always looked professional. She wore a beige pantsuit and brown high-heeled dress shoes, and her long, straight blonde hair hung below her shoulders. The thick mascara on her eyelashes accentuated her cat-like green eyes. She had silky smooth skin and full, glossy red lips. When she spotted Jim, Brenda waved and smiled warmly. Jim smiled and waved back.

"Hi, Jim," Brenda said, sitting in the lounge chair beside him. "I see you've already ordered me a coffee. Thanks."

"You're welcome, Brenda. I wasn't sure how you like it, so I picked up cream and sugar just in case."

"I prefer my coffee with milk or cream, no sugar. Thanks again."

"No problem."

"It's been a while since we've talked. How's your family, Jim?"

"Everyone's fine. Kristina is enjoying university, and Nic is graduating high school this year. It's hard to believe how fast kids grow up these days. It won't be long, and we'll be empty nesters. How are Mark and Jennifer?"

"They're great. Like Nicolas, Jennifer will graduate high school this year, and Mark has two more years to go. By the way, I'm sorry about the other night at Kelly's. Rusty had too much to drink, and he gets a little crazy sometimes. I hope Buck is okay."

"There's nothing to be sorry about, and I'm sure Buck has forgotten all about it by now. As you know, Rusty and Buck never get along and enjoy trying to get each other riled. Boys will be boys."

"I'm sure you didn't ask me here to discuss the weather. What's up, Jim?"

Jim cleared his throat, sipped his coffee, and told her the real reason for their meeting.

Brenda listened without saying a word. When Jim finished, she looked at him and softly said, "There's no need for a DNA test, Jim. It would only confirm that I was there. Yes, I was having an affair with Wayne Blackmore. It all started a few months ago at a seminar in Bangor. We tried to get together once or twice a week. I picked Buck's cabin because I knew it was vacant and secluded. Motels were out of the question because we're both well-known in the area. Although it was far from being the Ritz, we felt the cabin was the safest place. I thought I was falling in love with Wayne. He said he no longer loved his wife and planned to leave her. He wanted me to divorce Rusty so that we could be together. I told him that wasn't going to happen. You know Rusty, Jim, he would go crazy if I asked him for a divorce. Besides, Wayne and I hardly knew each other. Anyway, I told Wayne that Rusty had a volatile temper, and if he found out about our affair, there's no telling what he might do. That's when I came to my senses, Jim. I broke it off and told Wayne I wouldn't return. It hurt me to say it was over. I think he was devastated. Now, I realize how stupid I was for getting involved in the first place. Wayne was a real charmer and a very nice man. He gave me the love and attention I wasn't getting from Rusty. Jim, as God is my witness, I swear I didn't kill Wayne Blackmore. He was very much alive when I left the cabin that night."

"Do you have any idea who might have wanted him dead?"

"Not really, but he did mention that he had a large gambling debt his wife knew nothing about. Wayne said the people he owed the money to were scary. He told me they were getting impatient with his promises to pay that he wasn't keeping. Wayne said he was working on a plan that would pay them back.

"Do you have any idea what his plan entailed?"

"No, I don't. That's all Wayne would say."

"Did he ever mention who these people were? Any names, that sort of thing?"

"No names were ever mentioned, but I could tell he was pretty damn scared. He was getting paranoid because he believed someone was following him."

"I'm sorry to have to ask you this, Brenda, but I wouldn't be doing my job if I didn't ask. Do you or Rusty own a .38 caliber pistol?"

Brenda hesitated for a moment. "Yes, I owned a .38 caliber Lady Smith & Wesson."

"You mentioned you owned a .38 caliber Lady Smith & Wesson in the past tense. Does that mean you don't own it now?"

"A few weeks ago, someone broke into my car and stole it from the glove compartment. Rusty insisted that I keep it in my car for protection. He said, in my business, you never know what crazy maniac might want to target a female real estate agent. That thought scared the living daylights out of me."

"Did you report the theft?"

"I didn't, personally, but Rusty said not to worry—he would take care of it."

"Do you or Rusty know who might have taken the pistol?"

"I haven't got a clue. Rusty thought it might have been a druggie looking for anything of value that could be sold to buy drugs."

"Was anything else missing?"

"No. Just the gun."

"Was Rusty with you when the gun was purchased?"

"Yes, he was. I'm the registered owner, but Rusty paid for it. He said it was my Christmas gift. Some Christmas gift, huh."

"Do you remember the name of the gun shop?"

"I think it was called Old Town Gun Shop, in Old Town. It was just outside of town near a service station."

"I know the place. I've been there a few times on job-related matters. Does Rusty know about your affair with Wayne Blackmore?"

"If he does, he's never said anything. Although I think he may have suspected something."

"What makes you say that?"

"Once, when I got home a little later than usual after being with Wayne, he asked me where I'd been. I lied and told him I was working on a real estate deal. I said the showing went later than expected, and the clients loved the house and wanted to write up an offer immediately. He asked me why I hadn't called. I said I'd lost track of time, thought he might be in bed, and didn't wish to disturb him. He seemed to accept my explanation, but I'm not sure he believed me."

"I have one more question. Did you remember seeing Wayne Blackmore's car when you left the cabin that night?"

"Yes. As I was leaving, Wayne's car was still there. He originally planned to stay for several days, but since I wouldn't return, he decided to go home in the morning. He said he would talk to his wife and try to work things out."

Jim decided not to disclose that Wayne Blackmore's vehicle had been discovered in Pushaw Lake.

"Well, that's it for now, Brenda. Thank you for meeting with me. I appreciate you answering my questions, and I may need to talk to you again soon."

Jim handed Brenda his card and asked her to call if she thought of anything else.

They shook hands and left.

Walking back to the station, Jim was thinking. A gunshot to the middle of the forehead looked like a professional hit. If it were the Mafia or some other loan shark, why would they want to kill the "Golden Goose" before it laid the golden egg? That part didn't make sense—why kill someone before they paid the debt? There had to be an explanation!

CHAPTER 14

Friday morning, Jim and Buck drove to Bangor to attend Wayne Blackmore's funeral. A memorial service was scheduled for eleven in the chapel of the Rest-in-Peace funeral home. Wayne Blackmore's body had previously been cremated.

Since Buck was an amateur photographer, Jim had invited him to come along. His job was to snap pictures of attendees as they arrived and departed. They were looking for anyone who seemed suspicious or out of place.

As people left their vehicles and headed to the main entrance, Buck discreetly snapped pictures from the parking lot. He had a new digital camera with a telephoto lens. It was almost like being a sniper again. Instead of a rifle, he used a camera to sight his targets.

While Buck took pictures, Jim went inside and found a seat in the back row where he could observe the crowd. As his eyes scanned the room, he spotted two men with olive complexions and greasy salt-and-pepper hair. They wore dark business suits and looked uneasy, like a fish out of water. He didn't think they looked like real estate salespeople. Maybe it was his imagination, but if he had to guess, Jim could swear they looked more like gangsters—the stereotypes you saw in movies. He hoped that Buck had taken their pictures.

Donna Blackmore sat on the right side in the front row with her two sons, Billy and Bobby. She wore a stylish black dress and a wide-brimmed black hat. Throughout the service, she kept dabbing at her eyes with a tissue. Her boys sat like two stones in stunned silence, rubbing their eyes occasionally.

Office manager Carl Parker and his wife sat directly behind

Donna Blackmore. Janis Cromwell, the receptionist, and her husband sat beside the Parkers. The rest of the real estate staff were scattered throughout the chapel.

The preacher gave an uplifting sermon. He said death on earth was the beginning of life everlasting if you believed in our Lord Jesus Christ. He read from the scripture about walking through the valley of death and fearing no evil. For the most part, Jim found the sermon to be quite inspirational.

Before ending, the pastor looked straight at Donna and her two boys and said, "Mrs. Blackmore, Wayne is now with our Lord in heaven. Although he will be sadly missed, Wayne will be with you always in your thoughts, hearts, and memories—may his soul rest in peace. Amen. Please stand and repeat the Lord's Prayer." He began, "Our Father which art in heaven...."

After the Lord's Prayer had ended, the minister asked everyone to remain standing. A young female vocalist with an angelic voice began to sing "Amazing Grace," accompanied by a middle-aged man on the piano. Everyone joined in.

When the song ended, Carl Parker stepped up to the podium. "Mrs. Blackmore has asked me to give a brief eulogy." He cleared his throat and said, "Ladies and gentlemen, Wayne Blackmore was a great boss and a friend to all the staff at All-Star Realty. He will be sorrowfully missed by everyone who knew him." He looked at Donna Blackmore and her two sons and continued, "Wayne was a wonderful father to his sons, Billy and Bobby. He was a compassionate and charitable man who gave his time and worked hard on numerous committees to help make Bangor a better city to live in and raise our families." After a few more comments, he paused and looked at the ceiling. "Wayne, you are now at peace with the Lord in heaven above. May God bless your lovely wife, Donna, Billy, and Bobby, and give them the strength and courage to continue without you." He stepped down and returned to his seat.

Jim noticed that Parker failed to mention anything about Wayne Blackmore being a devoted and loving husband.

The preacher returned to the podium and said, "That concludes our service. Mrs. Blackmore has asked me to announce that you are all welcome to stay for refreshments and sandwiches. As you leave the chapel, turn right and take the stairs to the lower level. There is an elevator next to the stairway for those who wish to use it. Thank you, and may God bless you."

As the crowd began to disperse, Jim spoke briefly with Donna. She introduced him to her sons and thanked him for coming. He expressed his deepest sympathy and offered condolences to her and the boys. He said, "Sorry, I'm unable to stay for refreshments. Duty calls."

Jim said goodbye, and as he walked away, he noticed the two gangster types talking to Donna. From the expression on her face, she wasn't pleased to see them. He might have been imagining, but she looked pale and frightened.

As Jim slipped into the driver's seat, he noticed the two men coming out of the front entrance. They weren't staying for refreshments either. Buck took several close-up pictures as they headed toward their gleaming black Lincoln Town Car.

Buck was at the cabin by eight the morning after Wayne Blackmore's funeral service.

While at the Home Depot, he ordered kitchen cabinets, a stainless steel double sink, a refrigerator, a stove, a microwave, and a stackable washer/dryer. He also purchased bathroom fixtures, including an oversized acrylic shower that would replace the old bathtub. Buck had arranged to call Terry Wells when he was ready for the items to be delivered.

He was excited to start the renovations. Buck had ordered a wide plank floorboard called Antique Reclaimed Barn Board Natural from a local dealer. He was confident the new flooring would spruce up the old place.

Because the furniture was old and musty-smelling, for a reasonable fee, John's Junk Removal had recently cleared the cabin.

Now empty, working on the floor without moving furniture was much more manageable.

Buck started in the back bedroom, furthest away from the front entrance. At noon, he stopped for a beer and to eat a ham and cheese sandwich he had made before leaving the house. By mid-afternoon, he had finished the master bedroom and was enjoying a beer break when the truck from the flooring store arrived. The boards sat on a pallet covered with plastic to protect them from the weather. Buck went outside, signed a receipt, and returned to work.

After finishing the hallway and bathroom, Buck decided to call it a day. Just as he prepared to leave, he rolled up the Afghan rug he had kept for sentimental reasons. It was a gift to his grandfather for his seventy-fifth birthday. He noticed newer nails in several floorboards where the rug had been. Buck found it odd because no one had lived in the cabin since his grandfather had passed away almost eight years ago. It was getting late, and he was dead tired. He decided it could wait until Monday.

It had become routine for Buck and Jim to catch up and have a nightcap in the family room after Shawna and the kids had gone to bed.

Sipping on his whiskey, Jim said, "I'd like to thank you, B.J., for taking pictures at the Blackmore funeral, and I appreciate you putting them on a disc for me."

"You're welcome, Telly. I enjoyed the day off from working at the cabin."

"Listen to this! Before leaving, I sent a picture of each of the two greaseballs who attended Wayne Blackmore's funeral to see if they were in the NCIC database, and I got a hit. They're the Catalini brothers, Joe and Carmen. About two years ago, they were released from prison after spending several years behind bars for loan sharking and extortion. As I left the funeral home, I noticed them talking with Donna Blackmore, and she didn't look pleased to see them. She looked pale and frightened."

"Holy shit! Maybe they're back in business. Why else would they have gone to Blackmore's funeral?"

"I think I should visit Donna and try to find out what's happening."

"Good idea, Telly."

After Buck had gone to bed, Jim stayed in the family room and consumed a few extra drinks. At one in the morning, feeling no pain, he turned off the lights and stumbled up the stairs to bed.

That night Buck had another nightmare. This time it wasn't about Doreen. He was standing in an alley in New York City on a cold December morning, staring down at the lifeless body of Cheryl Jenkins. Tears were streaming down his face, and his eyes were blurry. He couldn't believe that she was dead. She had been so full of life, and he had always enjoyed her sense of humor. They had only been partners for a little over three years. A few disagreements had popped up during that time, but for the most part, they had gotten along well. Now, two weeks before Christmas, her two children were without their loving and caring mother. Her husband, John, a New York City firefighter, would have to face losing the love of his life. Buck was aware John knew they were in jobs where they put their lives on the line daily—but you never expected it to happen to you. Suddenly, the vision of Cheryl's killer came into view. He was laughing and pointing his gun at Buck. He said, "Now it's your turn to die, pig, just like your partner." As he was about to squeeze the trigger, Buck awoke in a panic. "No, no, no," he cried out.

He hoped he hadn't woken up the whole house. Buck tried, but he couldn't fall back to sleep. He tossed and turned until daybreak. Getting out of bed, Buck quietly got dressed and went for his morning jog. This time he didn't encounter Rusty Sykes.

CHAPTER 15

J im was at his desk by eight on Monday morning, reading notes
from his interview with Brenda Sykes. Was she telling the truth,
or did she know more about Wayne Blackmore's death than she
mentioned? His phone rang, interrupting his thoughts.

"Detective, Barkowsky."

"Good morning, Detective. It's Dr. Corey Chambers. I've got the
ballistics test results from the gun you sent over. Sorry, it's not the
murder weapon. It didn't match. I thought you'd like to know ASAP.
I'll send you the full report shortly."

"Okay, thanks, Doc. I appreciate the call."

"Goodbye, Jim. Have a nice day!"

"You, too. Goodbye."

After they had hung up, Jim sat in silence, thinking. I now
have two main suspects to consider—Brenda Sykes and Donna
Blackmore, and I can't rule out the Catalini brothers, and maybe
I can add a jealous husband—Rusty Sykes, to the list. Things are
getting interesting—if only I could find that damn murder weapon,
it would help.

Jim briefly met with officers Mark Talbot and Craig Walker at
nine. They had completed their calls to all the gun shops and were
awaiting the results.

Next, he met with Captain Timpano and Chief Durham. He
gave them the disappointing news from the crime lab and told
them about his interview with Brenda Sykes. He also mentioned
the information he read on the NCIC database about the Catalini
brothers.

His two superiors listened intently, and when Jim finished, Chief

Durham said, "Well, Jim, it certainly looks like you're making progress. The crime lab news didn't solve the murder weapon mystery. However, it sounds like you have a few suspects, but without the murder weapon, it will be hard to tie any of them to the crime. Do you know if Rusty reported his wife's gun stolen?"

"I haven't asked him about it yet. I thought I'd wait until we get the results from the gun shops to see if Brenda's name comes up as one of the purchasers."

"Do you think Rusty knows about his wife's infidelity?" Captain Timpano asked.

"I'm not sure, but he could have suspicions based on what Brenda told me during the interview."

"It's not too often we get a homicide in these parts. The media have been acting like sharks to the scent of blood. They want to know what's going on with the investigation. I can't hold them off forever. We'll have to call a news conference in a day or two and give them an update. I'll contact the Maine State Police and work with them to set it up. That should get those damn reporters off our backs for a little while. I even got a call from our illustrious mayor, Steve Smith, wanting to know what was happening. Sharon Cox, that persistent TV news reporter from Bangor, has called several times. I've kept her at bay so far, but she's tenacious as hell. She could drive a reformed alcoholic back to the bottle," the chief said with a half-hearted laugh.

"Tell me about it. The other day, she caught me coming out of the All-Star Realty building and shoved a mic in my face. I managed to get away by telling her the investigation was still in the early stages, and I told her I had nothing to say. I had to run to my car to escape her and several other reporters. They were like a pack of bloodhounds hot on the scent of an escaped convict."

"I've been thinking. Since Brenda said she purchased a .38 caliber pistol, we might want to consider getting a search warrant for the Sykes house, property, and vehicles," the captain said.

The chief nodded. "Good idea, Captain. Let's wait until we

receive the results from the gun shop search, and we can go from there. Is there anything else?"

"Nothing I can think of," Jim said.

"I don't have anything further," Tony replied.

"Okay. That's it," the chief said, "meeting adjourned."

By the time Buck reached the cabin, his curiosity was killing him. Since leaving on Saturday, he had been thinking about the new nails in the floorboards. Someone had been in the cabin since his grandfather's death, and they removed several floorboards and reinstalled the boards using new nails. Why?

Just as Buck decided to return to the cabin to start work, gravel crunched under tires coming down the driveway. In less than a minute, the Maine State Police dive team arrived, followed by a tow truck.

After saying hello to the three familiar faces and the tow truck driver, Buck excused himself and returned to work.

Before he could do anything, his cell phone rang. It was Jim.

"Hi, Telly," Buck said as he viewed the name on his screen.

"Hey, B.J.," Jim said. "Has the dive team and tow truck got there yet?"

"Yeah, they just arrived a few minutes ago."

"I'd like to be there, but it looks like I won't be able to make it."

"No problem. There's nothing you can do here anyway."

"You're right. See you tonight."

"Okay. See you!"

A short time later, Wayne Blackmore's vehicle was out of the water and headed to the crime lab for processing.

As he pried up each board, Buck's heart started beating a little faster. What would he find? Was there a dead body buried in the dirt?

"Don't be crazy, Buck. There's probably nothing to it," he said aloud.

After he had removed the last floorboard, Buck went and got

the flashlight from his toolbox. As he shone the light into the crawl space, the dirt looked freshly dug up and replaced. His curiosity was getting the best of him. He ran out to the shed and found a long-handled spade. Rushing back, he began to dig feverishly. After a few feet, Buck felt the shovel hit something soft. As he removed more dirt, the object began to take shape. Buck got down on his knees and started to dig with his hands. Once he had removed enough dirt, he saw a black bag that kids use to carry their hockey equipment. Buck was sure it didn't contain goalie pads and a jockstrap! With gloved hands, he unzipped the bag. What he saw shocked him. It wasn't body parts. The bag was loaded with clear plastic bags filled with white powder. As a former drug squad detective, he was sure it wasn't baking soda. Was it heroin, or was it cocaine?

"What the hell's going on here?" Buck asked the empty room.

He didn't want to remove the bag containing the suspected stash of drugs for fear of disturbing evidence. He slipped off his work gloves, pulled out his cell phone, and dialed. On the third ring, Jim answered.

"Hi, B.J., what's happening?"

"I know you said you were busy, but can you get away?"

"Why, what's up?"

"You'd better get your ass out to the cabin—now! You won't believe what I found buried under the living room floor."

"Shit, another body?"

"No. It looks like a hockey equipment bag filled with bags of white powder. I'm guessing it's not powdered milk or baking soda."

"Wow! Sit tight, partner. I'm on my way."

Jim arrived in less than thirty minutes.

Buck greeted him at the door, and together they walked to the opening on the living room floor. Buck shone his flashlight into the crawl space so Jim could look at the uncovered bag.

"My God, B.J., what the fuck's going on? Do you think this has any connection to Wayne Blackmore's murder?"

"Your guess is as good as mine. If it doesn't, then this is one hell of a coincidence."

"I hope you didn't touch anything. Sorry, that was stupid. I know as a detective, you know better."

"I still had my work gloves on when I unzipped the bag and didn't touch anything else. Then I called you."

"Good. Before we go any further, I'd better call this in and get a fingerprint expert and photographer out here."

While they waited, Jim updated Buck on the investigation.

"By the way," Jim said, "since Brad Strongman won't be around for a while, I was wondering if you might want to help me with the case. I want to get it solved before he returns. I could sure use your experience and expertise. When I spoke to the chief the other day, he approved it as long as we don't create a lot of attention. Since we're short-staffed and over budget, there won't be any compensation, but working together might be fun. What do you say, partner?"

"I appreciate your confidence, Telly, but as I said to Brad Strongman, I'm on vacation and prefer to stay that way."

"You could still be officially on sabbatical and act as my consultant. Think about it."

"This whole thing is getting more and more complicated each day. It's like a giant jigsaw puzzle with a lot of missing pieces. I admit it's starting to intrigue me. If I keep a low profile, you and I could work the case together. Maybe you could even teach me a trick or two."

Jim laughed. "I doubt that. I was hoping you could teach me a few tricks. We very seldom deal with a murder in our small town. After all, you're the big-city homicide detective and probably solved hundreds of cases."

Buck said with a modest grin, "I can't say I've solved hundreds of cases, but I've helped to solve a few. That's why they call us detectives, Telly. It's our job to detect things, put all the pieces together, and solve the puzzle. We became detectives because we like a challenge."

"I like a challenge just as much as the next guy. If we could work together, we might be able to crack this case a lot quicker. I value your opinion, Buck. If you have any ideas or theories, I'd appreciate you sharing them with me."

"I think Wayne Blackmore was into more than just real estate. He could've been a drug dealer and got into bed with the wrong people—or he could've stolen the drugs, intending to sell them to pay off his debt to the loan sharks," Buck said.

"What you're saying makes sense, Buck. The why may never be answered unless we find out who shot him."

"Once we find out who shot him, the reason should become clear. Is that what you're thinking, Telly?"

"That's what I'm thinking, B.J., my friend."

Changing the subject, Buck asked, "Have you been keeping track of the race for the White House?"

"Yeah, I've watched a bit of it on CNN. It looks like Donald and Hillary spend most of their time digging up dirt on each other rather than discussing the main issues," Jim said.

"Who do you think will win?" Buck asked.

"The polls are close, but Hillary has a slight lead. There's no telling who might win. The one thing I don't like is the Electoral College system. You could win the popular vote and lose the election. It doesn't make sense to me, but what do I know," Jim said.

"Yeah, you're right, but I don't think it's going to change anytime soon," Buck said.

"Have you decided who you're going to vote for?"

"I don't like either candidate. It might boil down to flipping a coin," Buck joked.

"Yeah, it's going to be a hard decision for me as well," Jim said. "I almost don't feel like voting, but I haven't missed casting my ballot since I was eligible to vote. That's what our democracy is all about. At least we have a say in who gets elected. Unfortunately, millions don't have that privilege in countries run by dictators."

"You've got that right. We can thank our lucky stars that we live in the good ole USA. Keeping our country free is one of the reasons I joined the Marines. Freedom doesn't come free—it takes sacrifice, and sometimes you've got to fight for it."

"That's for sure," Jim agreed.

They talked about sports, family, and fishing until the sound of tires on gravel announced a vehicle in the laneway. Doug Graham and Dan Evans pulled in a few seconds later, eager to start.

As they exited the car, Jim and Buck greeted them with smiles and handshakes.

Doug Graham chuckled and said, "You guys must like us. We can't keep meeting like this. The neighbors are gonna start talking."

"What neighbors?" Buck laughed. "Do you see any, Telly?"

As they headed toward the cabin, Jim said, "Well, at least it's not a stiff wasting away in the dirt, and thank God, there's no foul smell this time."

"Well, let's see what we've got," Dan said.

Buck led the way to the gaping hole in the floor, and Jim held the flashlight so they could view the evidence.

The two men gloved up and carefully lowered themselves into the crawl space. Doug took several pictures, and Dan checked the bag for prints. He found fingerprints on the carrying bag and a few more on the clear plastic bags containing the white powder.

"We've done all we can do here," Dan said. "Doug and I'll take the evidence to the crime lab for testing. I'm sure the test will confirm our suspicions the drug is heroin. We'll hold it until our superiors determine who will oversee the investigation. Depending on the tale the prints tell, I suspect the evidence may be turned over to the Maine DEA. Who knows, the federal DEA or the FBI might also get involved. Someone will keep you posted, Jim."

"Okay, guys, we'll leave it in your capable hands. It's been good seeing you again." Jim said.

Dan dropped the bag into the trunk. They shook hands with the two detectives, said goodbye, and drove off.

"B.J., my friend, we need to get the hell out of here, go home, and have a stiff drink or three or four."

"Sounds like a good idea, Telly. We might even find a few pieces to the puzzle. If not, we can have fun trying."

"Sounds like a plan. I'm dying of thirst," Jim said.

Trying to look serious but unable to keep a straight face, Buck asked, "Do you think we're becoming alcoholics?"

Jim laughed. "Nah, we just like to drink a lot."

Jim drove off while Buck locked the door. He'd had enough excitement for one day, and It was time to unwind.

At the family room bar, Jim threw ice into two glasses, poured them a generous shot of Crown Royal, and handed a glass to Buck.

"Well," Jim said, "it looks like we've got a real mystery on our hands, a lot of questions, but so far, very few answers."

"The first question is, who killed Wayne Blackmore? The second question is, who buried the bag? The third question is, are they connected?"

"At first, I thought the killer might have been the mystery woman who turned out to be Brenda Sykes. However, now I'm not so sure. Donna Blackmore had two million reasons, plus his infidelity, to want her husband dead. Those two things gave her a damn good motive. Next, I thought it might be a loan shark or a Mafia hitman. Now that the Catalini brothers are in the picture, maybe they killed Wayne Blackmore. Brenda said Wayne owed some scary people a lot of money. I'm not sure that makes sense. A dead man can't pay back a loan. Now, the new angle is the stash of drugs. Did Wayne Blackmore bury them, or did someone else put the drugs there? If the drugs were Blackmore's, where did he get them? Would he use the proceeds from their sale to repay his loan, or would he give the drugs to the loan sharks to pay off his debt? We have a lot of questions but no answers. The key to breaking this case wide open is still the murder weapon. If we can find that damn gun, it may lead to the killer."

"I agree. The gun is the missing piece to the puzzle," Buck said, downing the rest of his drink.

CHAPTER 16

The following morning, Jim met with Chief Durham and Captain Tony Timpano at eight. The Maine State Police, in conjunction with the Attorney General's Office and Chief Durham, had scheduled a ten a.m. press conference. It was to take place next door in the Municipal Building's Town Council Chambers. The purpose of the news conference was to update the Wayne Blackmore murder case. A question-and-answer period would follow.

Lieutenant John Butler represented the Maine State Police, while Assistant District Attorney Paul Prentice represented the Attorney General's Office. Their meeting before the press conference was to prepare answers to the questions they were anticipating because they didn't want to be caught flat-footed.

Everyone agreed it was premature to disclose yesterday's new wrinkle—the bag they believed to be heroin. Once the fingerprint report from the crime lab arrived, it would give them a better idea of their next move. Since drugs were involved, the Maine Drug Enforcement Agency would probably be assigned the investigation.

At 9:55 a.m., Chief Durham, Jim, Tony Timpano, John Butler, and Paul Prentice entered the council chambers. The chief sat in the middle, Jim sat to the chief's right and Tony to his left. Each man had a microphone. They had agreed to let Chief Durham handle the press conference, along with Jim and Tony. The other two representatives decided to observe the proceedings from seats in the front row.

The room buzzed with anticipation. There must have been twenty-five or thirty reporters from newspapers and TV stations locally and other towns and cities throughout the state eagerly awaiting their arrival.

At 10:00 a.m. sharp, Chief Durham said, "May I have your attention, please." As the room fell silent, the chief cleared his throat and took a sip of water. With all eyes glued to him, he said, "Good morning. I'm Chief John Durham of the Orono PD. I'll read a brief statement, after which the floor will be open to questions. On Saturday morning, the 9th day of April, the body of a Caucasian male was discovered at a vacant cabin on Pushaw Lake. The corpse, in an advanced state of decomposition, had no identification. His watch, ring, credit cards, and cash were all missing. The Medical Examiner, Dr. Corey Chambers, estimated that the victim had been deceased for approximately seven to ten days. After gathering and examining evidence at the crime scene, the victim's death has been ruled a homicide. The body was taken to the crime lab in Augusta, where an autopsy was performed. No fingerprints of the murder victim turned up in the State of Maine or federal databases. Dental records positively identify the victim as forty-seven-year-old Wayne Daniel Blackmore. Mr. Blackmore was the owner of All-Star Realty, Inc., in Bangor. Detective Jim Barkowsky will now take your questions. Before we start, I suggest you don't all speak at once. Raise your hand, and we'll get to you one at a time. We ask that you identify yourself by name and the media you represent. I'll now turn things over to Detective Barkowsky."

"Thank you, Chief Durham. Good morning and welcome everyone."

Several reporters raised their hands and waved frantically to attract Jim's attention.

"Go ahead," Jim said, pointing to a woman in the front row.

"I'm Grace Felton from The Maine Campus in Orono. Do you have any suspects at this time?"

"We have a few leads we're working on, but it's too early in the investigation to give out specific details or name names."

Next, Jim pointed to a familiar face.

"I'm Sharon Cox from WABI Channel 5 TV in Bangor. Detective, have you determined the caliber of the gun used to kill Mr. Blackmore, and have you found the murder weapon?"

"Yes, the gun was a .38 caliber. We have not found the murder weapon but are confident it will turn up soon."

Jim pointed to a man in the second row.

"I'm Scott Patterson from WLBZ Channel 2 TV in Bangor."

"Detective Barkowsky, can you tell us what Mr. Blackmore was doing in that cabin?"

"Well, Scott, that's what our investigation is still trying to determine. That's all I can tell you at this time." Jim didn't want to disclose that Wayne Blackmore was having an affair.

"Next," Jim said, pointing to a lady in the back row.

"I'm Anne Watson with The Portland Times."

"Do you know if Mr. Blackmore was alone in the cabin when he was murdered? Excluding his killer, of course."

A few people snickered.

"We're still trying to determine that, Anne. As the investigation continues, we will keep the media informed."

Before another reporter could raise their hand, Sharon Cox asked, "Do you feel confident that Mr. Blackmore's killer will be caught and brought to justice?"

"Yes, Ms. Cox, I am confident that Wayne Blackmore's murderer will be apprehended and brought to justice. If you have further questions, Ms. Cox, please raise your hand and wait your turn like everyone else."

Her face reddened as several reporters gave her the evil eye for her intrusion.

Jim quickly turned away and pointed at another reporter, a heavy-set, middle-aged woman at the back of the room. "Next question, please."

"I'm Barbara Campbell with the Sun Journal in Lewiston. "I have two questions. Do you have any theories about who might have wanted to kill Mr. Blackmore, and do you think he was killed for his watch, ring, money, and credit cards?"

"Sorry, Barbara, I can't answer that question. All I can say is that we're looking into all possibilities. As we follow the evidence, I'm confident it will lead to Mr. Blackmore's killer and the reason for his murder."

The question-and-answer period continued for another twenty minutes.

Finally, Jim said, "That's it for now, folks. We assure you we are doing everything possible to find Mr. Blackmore's killer and bring whoever murdered him to justice. On behalf of the Maine State Police, the Attorney General's Office, and the Orono Police Department, we thank you for your time and patience. We will issue press releases to keep you informed of any new developments. Thanks again, and have a pleasant day!"

John Butler and Paul Prentice said goodbye and left after the press conference had ended.

As the Orono police officers stood to leave, the crowd became noisy and disgruntled.

A male voice griped, "Thanks a lot for nothing."

A female reporter shouted, "It doesn't sound like you've made much progress finding Mr. Blackmore's killer."

When they had retreated to Chief Durham's office, the chief said, "That went over like a lead balloon."

"Yeah," Jim agreed, "they weren't too happy. It sounds like the natives are getting restless, and I don't think the news conference did much to appease them."

Hot under the collar, Captain Timpano said, "Reporters never understand that not everything can be disclosed. They don't understand that giving them certain information too soon could hamper the investigation. They're all trying to beat each other for the big scoop. It would be nice if they could leave us alone and let us do our damn jobs."

"I agree," the chief said. "We'll have to ignore the media for now and carry on. What's your next move, Jim?"

"The information from the gun shops is starting to trickle in. We'll see if it gives us any leads and go from there."

"Okay, gentlemen, that's it for now. Keep me updated."

After lunch, Jim decided to take a little trip. The five miles took less than fifteen minutes. He had decided to check out the Old Town Gun Shop, where Brenda Sykes said Rusty had purchased the .38 caliber pistol for her.

The State of Maine does not require a permit to purchase, register, or license a rifle, shotgun, or handgun. Dealers must record all firearm sales, rentals, or loans, and the record is required to show the purchaser's or recipient's name and address along with the firearm's make, caliber, and serial number.

Jim identified himself and showed the young man at the counter his badge. After he explained the reason for his visit, the clerk asked Jim to follow him into the office. He sat before a computer and typed the name Brenda Jane Sykes. A few seconds later, a document appeared on the screen. The clerk clicked his mouse, and the information began to print. When the printer stopped, he handed Jim the copy.

He thanked the clerk and headed to his car. Before leaving, he sat behind the steering wheel and studied the information. It showed the name and address of the purchaser, the make, model, serial number, and caliber of the pistol. The purchase date was December 19, 2012. It was a .38 caliber Lady Smith & Wesson, exactly as Brenda had said.

When Jim returned to the station, he contacted Craig Walker and Mark Talbot and asked them to meet in his office at nine the following day to review the gun shop results.

CHAPTER 17

All the reports were completed. There were seventy-nine .38 caliber pistols sold in the gun shops surveyed within the past five years.

As Jim reviewed the names of the buyers from each shop, he didn't see the name Brenda Jane Sykes on the report from the Old Town Gun Shop. That shop was on Mark Talbot's contact list. Why is her name missing? Does Rusty have anything to do with it?

Jim was surprised to see the name Wayne Daniel Blackmore on the report from a Bangor gun shop. Donna Blackmore had mentioned that her husband owned a handgun, but she didn't know the make or caliber.

When he finished, Jim said, "The next step is for you to call all the gun owners and confirm whether or not they still possess the firearms. As I mentioned in our previous meeting, you must pick up the guns, tag them, and, once collected, deliver them to the crime lab for ballistics testing. Craig, Wayne Blackmore's name is on one of your lists. I'll take care of it. It's time I paid another visit to Mrs. Blackmore. That's it for now. Thanks."

After Craig and Mark left, Jim looked up the number and called the Old Town Gun Shop.

"Good morning, Old Town Gun Shop," a cheerful male voice said.

"Good morning. I'm Detective Barkowsky from the Orono PD. Recently, we asked for a copy of all .38 caliber pistols sold by Old Town Gun Shop within the past five years to be emailed to us. Do you know who was responsible for preparing that list?"

"Yes, Detective, it was me. My name is Peter Todd, and I met you the other day when you came into the shop for some information."

" Sorry, Peter, I forgot to ask your name. When we met, you gave me the purchase information for a .38 caliber Lady Smith & Wesson registered to Brenda Jane Sykes. Do you remember?"

"Yes, I remember."

"I'm curious why the information wasn't on the email list."

"I'm sorry, Detective, I thought you knew. One of your patrol officers came by the other day and told me not to put it on the list. When I asked him why he gave me a threatening glare and told me not to include it if I valued my health."

"Did you happen to catch his name or badge number?"

"Sorry, I didn't. It all happened so fast. The officer caught me completely off guard, and I didn't even think to look."

"Can you describe the officer to me?"

"Yeah, he looked mean. He was tall and muscular, with a crew cut. His hair was an unusual color, and it looked almost orange."

"Would reddish-orange describe his hair color?"

"Yeah, that's what it looked like."

"Thanks, Peter. I appreciate your help."

"I hope I'm not gonna get into trouble by telling you."

"Don't worry, Peter. You won't get into trouble. I'll take care of it. Thanks again. Goodbye."

Jim hung up and stared into space. Rusty, that bastard, now he's interfering with a police investigation.

Earlier, he remembered seeing Rusty in the building. He left his desk and walked down the hallway to the patrol officer's room. Rusty sat in front of a computer screen, drinking coffee and talking on his cell phone. It sounded like he was speaking with Brenda. When he saw Jim, he said, "I gotta go," and abruptly ended the conversation.

"Rusty, could I speak to you for a minute in my office, please?"

"What about?" Rusty asked. He looked agitated.

"It'll only take a minute, and I'd rather not discuss it here."

"Okay, I'll be right there."

Jim went back to his office and waited—and waited. It took ten minutes before Rusty walked through the door.

That bastard is playing games, trying to get me riled.

"Come in, Rusty. Take a seat, " Jim said, appearing calm, but he was boiling inside.

When Rusty sat down, Jim said, "I'm sure you're aware that in the Wayne Blackmore investigation, we're doing a canvass of all gun shops in the area. We're checking purchasers of all .38 caliber pistols sold within the last five years. As you may know, a .38 caliber bullet killed Wayne Blackmore, and one name was missing when we received the Old Town Gun Shop list."

"Oh. What name was that?"

"Your wife's name—but you already know that, right?"

"What do you mean I already know that?"

"By removing Brenda's name from the list, you're withholding and tampering with evidence in a murder investigation. As a cop, you know those are serious charges. I understand that you hinted there might be consequences if the clerk didn't remove Brenda's name from the list."

Losing his cool, Rusty shouted, "I did no such thing! It's his word against mine. What the hell do you intend to do about it?"

"Before we go any further, we'd better visit the chief and let him decide what to do about it. You should tell your side of the story in his presence—and you'd better change your attitude, or I'll cite you for insubordination."

"Go ahead and cite me, you jerk. I don't give a shit."

Rusty's blood pressure had risen into the stratosphere. He jumped to his feet and headed for the door—Jim hot on his heels.

Rusty barged into Chief Durham's office without knocking. The chief looked surprised, and he could sense something was wrong. He said, "Please close the door and sit down. Now, what's this all about, gentlemen?"

Before Jim could get a word out, Rusty started ranting and raving about how Jim was on his case about withholding evidence.

"Calm down, Rusty," the chief said sternly. "Don't say another word until I ask you to speak. What's this all about, Jim?"

Jim cleared his throat and said, "When I interviewed Brenda Sykes recently, she admitted owning a .38 caliber pistol. She told me it was stolen from her car in the past few weeks. The gun was purchased from the Old Town Gun Shop on December 19, 2012. Rusty paid for the gun, which was registered in Brenda's name. I visited the shop a few days ago, and they gave me a copy of the purchase information. Yesterday, Rusty stormed into the shop, and according to the clerk, he demanded that Brenda's name come off the list. Rusty hinted there would be consequences if the clerk didn't comply. Also, Chief, I wish to cite Rusty for insubordination toward a superior officer."

"Is what Jim just said true, Rusty?"

Rusty thought for a few seconds, then said, "I…I guess it's pretty much true, Chief."

The chief was starting to lose his patience. "Dammit, Rusty, what do you mean it's pretty much true? Is it true, or isn't it true?"

"Yeah, it's true. I was tryin' to protect Brenda. She had nothin' to do with the murder of Wayne Blackmore, and she didn't even have a gun. As Jim said, her gun was stolen before the murder was committed. Knowin' Jim, he's probably gonna try and pin it on Brenda. I won't let that happen."

"Rusty, it's not up to you to try to stop anything from happening. Like any good detective, Jim's job is to follow the evidence and see where it leads. If Brenda is innocent, I'm sure the evidence will exonerate her. For now, she will remain on our suspect list until proven otherwise. I will not tolerate insubordination under my command. Do you understand?"

"Yes, Chief. I didn't withhold evidence on purpose, and I didn't mean to be insubordinate to Detective Barkowsky. It's just that I lost my temper in the heat of the moment. I spoke before thinkin'. I apologize. All I'm askin' is that you give me the benefit of the doubt."

"I'm sorry, Rusty. What you've done is inexcusable, and it's grounds for dismissal. There's no benefit of the doubt. However, under the circumstances, with the stress that you and Brenda are under, you weren't thinking clearly. I will suspend you for one month without pay for trying to withhold evidence and one month without pay for insubordination to a superior officer. You will have time to reflect on your actions, allowing me to investigate this matter further. You must realize that no police officer is above the law. Get out of here before I change my mind and fire you."

CHAPTER 18

Arriving home shortly after his suspension, Rusty was madder than a provoked hornet. Smoking pot, he was sprawled out on the living room couch while a muted gangster movie played on the large-screen TV. He wasn't watching the film because Rusty's thoughts were on Jim Barkowsky. *That asshole cost me two months' pay, and he almost got me fired. Somehow I'll get even with that backstabbing son of a bitch.*

His thoughts were interrupted when Brenda arrived home and yelled, "Rusty, I saw your car in the driveway. Are you here?"

"Yeah, I'm in the livin' room," he shouted.

As she entered the room, seeing what he was up to, Brenda scolded, "What the hell are you doing smoking weed again? You promised that you had quit."

"Yeah, whatever. It's none of your fuckin' business, anyway."

"You don't have to get so hostile."

"If I'm hostile, as you call it, it's because of you whorin' around with that real estate guy."

"We've gone through that a hundred times. I told you what happened, and I've told you I'm sorry. What else do you want me to do? It would never have happened if you'd paid a little attention to me and were more of a caring, loving husband."

"How can I be a carin', lovin', fuckin' husband when you're never here?"

"You know damn well that real estate is not a nine-to-five job. I do what I have to do to help us pay the bills. If you didn't spend so much money on pot and God knows what other drugs, maybe I wouldn't have to work so hard."

"It's because of you I almost got fired. The chief suspended me for two fuckin' months without pay. I stuck my neck out tryin' to protect your ass from becomin' a suspect in your lover's murder, and this is the thanks I get?"

"Well, you didn't have to do that—I didn't kill anyone."

"How the hell am I supposed to know that?"

"I would have needed a gun, and my gun was stolen. Don't you remember?"

"Whatever!"

Just then, they heard their teenagers coming through the front door.

Mark entered the living room and said, "Hey, Dad, why are you home so early?"

Before Rusty could answer, Brenda said, "He's taking some time off—a little vacation."

Jennifer wrinkled up her nose. "Gross, Dad. You're smoking pot again."

"It's just a little for medicinal purposes, my dear," Rusty said with a silly grin. "Doctor's orders, it's for my bad back, and that's why I'm on vacation."

Buck was stunned when he went out to his truck earlier that morning. All four tires had been slashed, and someone had spray-painted a message on the white surface along the driver's side. In bright red letters, it read: "FUCK OFF ASSHOLE."

Buck stood for a few minutes, frozen in his tracks. Then he got fighting mad, and his blood began to boil. Only one name came to mind—Rusty Sykes!

Staring at his damaged truck, he yelled, "Okay, if you want to play games, Rusty, then game on."

After taking a few deep breaths, he managed to calm down. He decided to call Jim and get his take on the situation.

As Jim's phone rang, he saw Buck's name flash on his screen. "Hey, Buck, what's happening, man?"

"Where are you, Telly?"

"I'm in my car on the way to Bangor. I have another interview with Donna Blackmore. Why?"

Buck told him about his truck. Then he said, "Before I go and beat the shit out of Rusty, I thought we should talk. Lucky for Rusty, with four flat tires, I won't be going anywhere."

"Take it easy, buddy. I'll be home in a few hours. Sit tight. Don't do anything you're going to regret. Promise you'll wait for me."

"Okay."

"Good. I'll see you soon."

The spectacular 1700s classic reproduction colonial home was nestled on a two-acre private lot in an exclusive Bangor neighborhood. There was an attached three-car garage to the right of the impressive front entrance.

Jim slid out of his car, taking in the view. He slowly strolled to the large covered front porch and punched the doorbell. While waiting, he surveyed the front yard. The grounds were immaculately manicured and professionally landscaped. The long, circular, cobblestone driveway had room to park at least twenty vehicles. Very impressive!

Looking stressed, Donna Blackmore opened the door, smiled slightly, and said, "Detective Barkowsky, it's so nice to see you again. Please come in."

"It's nice to see you as well, Mrs. Blackmore."

"Please, Detective, call me Donna. Mrs. Blackmore was Wayne's mother."

"I was admiring your immaculate grounds and beautiful house, Donna."

"Unfortunately, it won't be the same without Wayne. It was his pride and joy. He designed it and had it custom-built several years ago."

She led Jim through a spacious front entrance with gleaming white marble flooring and an elegant crystal chandelier hanging from the foyer ceiling. A large eat-in kitchen on his right appeared to have all the bells and whistles: granite countertops, cherry wood cabinets, ceramic flooring, and stainless steel appliances. On his left, he viewed a dining room with expensive dark mahogany furniture. Next to the dining room, he paused to take in Wayne Blackmore's spacious office. He saw a large, dark oak desk with a matching side table that contained a desktop computer and printer. A high-back brown executive chair sat behind the desk, and two captain's chairs with dark-brown leather seats faced the desk. On the wall behind the desk, Jim could see the smiling faces of a family portrait. A beige file cabinet stood against the back wall to the left of the desk, and various books filled shelves mounted on the wall. A few outdoor paintings of scenery and animals were scattered throughout the room.

Catching up to Donna, Jim followed her into a cozy family room with gleaming light oak flooring. A large patterned wine-colored Oriental rug lay in front of a plush off-white leather couch. The room was completed by two matching leather chairs, a contrasting chocolate brown leather recliner, a glass-top coffee table, and matching end tables. Similar paintings to those seen in the office hung on the walls throughout the family room.

Across from the sitting area, a large-screen TV overhung the mantle of a red-brick, wood-burning fireplace. Double garden doors led to what appeared to be a cedar deck overlooking a kidney-shaped swimming pool and a private wooded backyard.

Jim sat on one of the leather chairs.

"You've got a beautiful home, Donna."

"Thank you, Detective. It's too bad Wayne will no longer be here to enjoy it with the boys and me. I've got a fresh pot of coffee brewing in the kitchen. Would you like a cup?"

"Yes, please. Black, no sugar, would be fine."

"I'll be right back."

Jim noticed that Donna looked tired. She had dark circles under her eyes, and her voice sounded weak and strained.

Jim fished out a notepad and pen from his suit pocket, ready to write.

When she returned, she handed him his mug and sat on the couch.

"Has anything new come up with the investigation, Detective?"

"Yes, Donna, a few things have come to light since we last spoke. The mystery woman has been identified. Her name is Brenda Sykes. She's a real estate sales representative at Big River Realty in Orono. She and your late husband met this past January at a seminar in Bangor, and they have had a relationship for the last few months. For your information, her husband, Russell Sykes, is a member of our police force."

"Her husband works on your police force? Does he know of his wife's involvement with my late husband?"

"Yes, he does."

"Is she a suspect in Wayne's murder, Detective?"

"Yes, but when I interviewed Brenda Sykes, she swears your husband was alive the last time she saw him."

"Do you think she's lying? Do you think her husband could be involved?"

"At this stage in the investigation, I don't have the answers to those questions. Mrs. Sykes said she owned a .38 caliber pistol, but it was stolen from her car's glove box a few weeks before the murder."

"That sounds like a cooked-up story."

"It could be. However, without the murder weapon, we don't have any proof. Finding the gun is the key to solving your husband's murder."

"Is there anything else?"

"Since our last conversation, the gun shop search revealed that your husband's gun was a Glock .38 caliber pistol."

"As I mentioned in our first meeting, I knew Wayne had a handgun, but I didn't know the make or caliber."

"The first time we met, you told me your husband may have kept his gun in his car's glove compartment. You were right Wayne did keep it in his car. On a hunch, we decided to have the Maine

State Police dive team check the lake, and they found his vehicle, and In the glove compartment, they found his Glock pistol. After a ballistics analysis, the crime lab called and informed me that your husband's gun is not the murder weapon."

"Maybe it was the gun owned by Brenda Sykes that killed Wayne. That's what I think."

"You could be right, but we have no proof until we find that gun. When I interviewed Brenda Sykes, she told me Wayne had mentioned he owed a lot of money to bad people. She said they were getting impatient and were pressing him for the money. She said that Wayne appeared to be on edge and scared. He told her you didn't know about his debt. She also said that your husband seemed paranoid, and he mentioned that he thought someone was following him."

"That's news to me. Wayne and I were always open about our finances. However, Wayne used to take overnight trips to Boston to see a friend. He was a big sports fan. Wayne said they would go to baseball, basketball, hockey, and football games, depending on the time of year. Do you think he was going to Boston to gamble or to bet on sports?"

"That's what we would like to find out. From what Brenda Sykes told me, it would appear the money Wayne owes is to a loan shark, and he must have borrowed it to cover his gambling losses. Before I forget, would you happen to know his friend's name, phone number, and address in Boston?"

"Sorry, Wayne never mentioned any name I can remember, and he did a good job hiding it from me if he went there to gamble. However, I noticed that he seemed stressed out and nervous lately, which could account for his irritability if he thought someone was following him."

"Since we last spoke, Mr. Frank Zubba from Global World Insurance called to inform me that you are the beneficiary of a two million dollar insurance policy on your husband's life. Are you aware of the policy?"

"Yes. Wayne wanted to ensure that if anything happened to him, the boys and I would not have to worry about finances. Are you thinking what I think you're thinking, Detective?"

"What do you think I'm thinking?"

"I killed my husband or had someone kill Wayne for the money."

"Did you?"

Instantly angry, she said, "I'm not even going to answer that ridiculous question. If there's nothing else, Detective, I've got things to do."

"I have one more question. Two men attended your husband's funeral. They seemed uneasy, out of place, as if they didn't belong there. They wore dark business suits, had olive complexions, and greasy salt-and-pepper hair. I'd say they were in their mid-fifties. They looked like they could be brothers. I saw you talking with them as I was leaving. Do you know who they are?"

The blood drained from Donna's face. She paused for a moment as if pondering the question. "That day is pretty much a blur. I talked to many people. Most of them expressed their sympathy and offered their condolences. If I remember correctly, those two men said they were my late husband's business associates. They told me Wayne was a good man, expressed their condolence, shook my hand, and left. That's all I can recall."

"Have you ever seen them before?"

"No, I haven't. That's the first time I laid eyes on them."

"A fellow police officer was taking pictures of all the attendees at your husband's funeral. We were searching for anyone who looked out of place. When we spotted those two, we thought they were worth checking. We submitted their pictures to a criminal database and got a hit. They are the Catalini brothers, Carmen and Joe. They have criminal records as long as your arm and spent several years in the slammer for loan sharking and extortion. They were released about two years ago and currently live in Boston. Through the Boston Police Department, we have determined they belong to the Boston Mafia—the Morano crime family. We believe they are back in business and suspect they are the ones who covered your husband's gambling debt."

"Should I be concerned, Detective? Do you think they will come after me for Wayne's debt?"

"We're not sure. By attending your husband's funeral, it looked like they were sizing you up. If they contact you asking for payment, please call me immediately. In the meantime, sit tight and try not to worry."

"Now you've got me scared."

"Sorry, that was not my intention. That's it for now, Donna. Thanks for your time and the coffee."

"I'll walk you out."

"That won't be necessary. I'll see myself out, thank you. Have a good day!"

CHAPTER 19

After Detective Barkowsky had left, tears began to flow. Donna had never cried so hard before.

She had not been honest with him. The Catalini brothers had indeed threatened her. They said Wayne owed them one hundred thousand dollars for a gambling debt. Donna told them she didn't have that kind of money. They said if she didn't come up with the full payment within one week, she and her boys could have an accident. That's when she broke down and told them about the two-million-dollar life insurance policy. They gave Donna a Cayman Island account number into which she was to deposit five hundred thousand dollars. Joe Catalini warned her not to contact the police or else. She got the message. The brothers did not come out and say they had murdered Wayne, but in her mind, there was no doubt—they were the ones who had shot him. She prayed that wouldn't happen to her and her boys.

Yesterday, Frank Zubba of Global World Insurance called to tell her they had confirmation that Wayne's death was not a suicide and a certified check for two million dollars would be delivered within a few days by registered mail.

Donna felt guilty for not telling Detective Barkowsky about her conversation with the Catalini brothers. Just as she was about to call him, Donna heard Billy and Bobby enter the house. She dried her eyes, composed herself, and went to greet them.

When Jim arrived back at the house, Buck was standing near his truck, talking on his cell phone with a tow truck operator, making arrangements for his truck to be towed to a tire shop.

As Buck hung up, Jim said, "Wow, someone did a number on your tires."

Buck said, "Not someone—Rusty!"

"Let's not jump to conclusions, Buck. Unless you can prove it was Rusty, we'd better tread lightly."

"What more proof do we need? You heard him the other night telling me it wasn't over. Who the hell else could it be?"

"Granted, it probably was Rusty, but unless someone saw him do it, we don't have a leg to stand on. We can't accuse him without proof."

"It's so fucking frustrating knowing he did it but unable to prove it. I bet he's sitting at home laughing his brainless head off."

"You're right. Rusty is at home, and he's been suspended for two months without pay. I'll fill you in tonight."

Twenty minutes later, a flatbed tow truck pulled into the driveway. The driver stepped down and whistled when he saw Buck's truck.

"Man," he said, "what crazy idiot went after your truck?"

"Some sick fuck without a brain."

The driver chuckled. Then he hooked the truck up and winched it onto the flatbed. He secured it with chains and said, "I'm ready to go if you are?"

"See you later, Telly,"

He climbed into the truck, and they drove away.

A couple of hours later, Buck returned, a little lighter in the wallet—his truck sitting on four brand new tires.

As he entered the front door, Jim yelled, "I'm in the family room. Grab a beer and join me."

Buck stopped in the kitchen and plucked a beer from the fridge. "How did you make out?"

"The tires weren't repairable—thanks to Rusty."

"To be safe, from now on, you'd better put your truck in the garage. While you were gone, I cleaned the junk from the third bay.

Your truck should fit in nicely, and here's a remote door opener you can use." Jim handed it to Buck.

"Thanks, Telly, I appreciate it. With that maniac on the loose, it's better to be safe than sorry."

"What about the paint job?"

"Luckily, the paint was washable. The tire guys did me a big favor and washed it off, and the truck looks as good as new."

"That's great! It's much better than paying for a new paint job."

"You got that right, Telly. Here's to better days. Cheers!"

"I'll drink to that, brother. Cheers."

Jim took a few minutes to tell Buck why Rusty had been suspended.

When Jim finished, Buck said, "Why am I not surprised? Maybe Chief Durham will reconsider and fire that idiot."

"We can only hope," Jim said.

CHAPTER 20

The doorbell rang, and Shawna yelled, "I've got it."
When Shawna opened the door, she was surprised to see a face she hadn't seen in years.

"Hi, Shawna. I'm Terry Wells. Is Buck here?"

"Terry, I almost didn't recognize you. It's nice to see you. Come in. I'll get Buck for you."

She entered the family room, where Jim and Buck were drinking beer and watching a Red Sox game.

"Sorry to interrupt, guys. Buck, you've got a visitor."

"That's strange. Not many people know I'm staying here. Who is it?"

"It's Terry Wells."

"Terry Wells? I wonder what he wants? "

Shawna escorted Terry into the room, made an excuse, and left.

"Hi, Terry," Buck said as they shook hands. "You remember Jim Barkowsky from high school, don't you?"

"Hi, Terry," Jim said, shaking hands. "Long time no see."

"Nice to see you again, Jim."

"What's up, Terry? Are you here about my Home Depot order?" Buck asked.

"No, but your order is ready to be delivered whenever you're ready, Buck."

Perplexed, Buck asked, "What is it then?"

"I've been thinking about our conversation when you were at the store, and I didn't tell you the truth about the night Doreen died."

"Oh," Buck said, "what didn't you tell me, Terry?"

Terry's eyes moistened, tears ran down his cheeks, and he began to tremble. He paused to compose himself, then slowly said, "I followed Rusty. He was staggering because he was stoned on pot. Downriver, away from the party, I saw Doreen standing by the water arguing with Brenda Blake, Rusty's girlfriend. I heard Brenda say, 'You and Buck think you're too good to hang with us.' The next thing I know, Brenda grabs Doreen's necklace, rips it off her neck, picks up a rock, and hits her square on the forehead. Doreen lost her balance and stumbled backward into the river. When Rusty and I arrived, Doreen was swept away by the current. Rusty sobered up in a hurry when he saw me. He looked me straight in the eye and said, 'You didn't see anything, Wells. If you ever say one word, you're dead meat. Knowing Rusty, I'm sure he meant it, so I turned and ran. That scene has haunted me all these years. I decided it was time to stop being a chicken and tell you what really happened that night. I'm so sorry, Buck. I should've had the courage to tell the police this story back then. I'm so ashamed. Can you ever forgive me, Buck? I don't know if I'll ever forgive myself."

Terry flopped onto the couch, bent over, buried his face in his hands, and wept again.

Buck went over and sat down beside him. He put his arm around Terry's shoulder and said, "It's okay, Terry. Don't worry. I forgive you. It took a lot of guts to do what you just did."

Jim sat in stunned silence. When his brain began to function again, he said, "Terry, would you be willing to come to the station tomorrow and give us a recorded statement of what you said tonight?"

Terry, still distraught, gave a brief nod and stammered, "Yes, I…I will, Jim."

After Terry had left, Shawna returned and asked, "What was that all about?"

"Shawna, you're not going to believe this, and you'd better sit down," Jim said. "Terry just told us a story about the night Doreen Warren died. He said he witnessed Brenda Blake grabbing Doreen's necklace, hitting her head with a rock, and watching Doreen fall into the river and get swept away."

"Oh, my God, how awful. Why did Terry wait so long?"

"Because Rusty threatened to beat the shit out of him if he told anyone about what he saw," Buck said. "When we met at the Home Depot, we talked about what happened to Doreen that night. I told him I'd always suspected her death wasn't an accident. He started to feel guilty for not coming forward back then. Tonight, Terry said it's been bothering him all these years, and it was time he told the truth. He agreed to go to the police station in the morning and give a statement about what he witnessed."

Terry arrived shortly after nine the following day. Jim greeted him as Elsie Brody ushered Terry into his office.

"Good morning, Terry."

"Good morning, Jim."

"Can I get you a coffee?"

"Yes, please, Jim. Cream, no sugar, would be great."

In a few minutes, Jim returned with two coffees. He handed Terry his and said, "Thanks for coming in, Terry. I've arranged to meet with Chief Durham and Captain Tony Timpano in the chief's office. That's where we'll record your statement."

"Okay, Jim. I must admit I'm very nervous. I hardly slept at all last night."

"There's nothing to be nervous about, Terry. Just try to relax, and everything will be fine. Chief Durham and Captain Timpano are on your side."

In the chief's office, Jim introduced Terry to Chief Durham and Captain Timpano. The chief thanked Terry for coming in, explained the procedure and asked if he had any questions.

"No, Chief Durham, I don't have any questions."

"Are you ready to start, Terry?" Jim asked.

Terry nodded. "Yes, Jim, I'm ready."

Jim turned on the recorder. He stated the date, time, location, and names of everyone present. He gave the witness's full name and said the following declaration was regarding Miss Doreen Patricia Warren's death on Saturday, June 25th, 1988.

Jim asked, "Mr. Wells, is the information you are about to provide the truth, the whole truth and nothing but the truth, so help you, God."

"Yes, it is."

Jim said, "Mr. Wells, please describe what you witnessed on the night of June 25th, 1988."

Terry was nervous, but he spoke slowly and clearly. He reiterated the same story he had told Buck and Jim the previous evening. When Terry finished, Jim recorded the date and time the declaration had concluded. When Jim stopped the recorder, Terry breathed a loud sigh of relief.

"Great job, Terry. Thanks!" Jim said.

Chief Durham and Captain Timpano thanked him as well.

Terry was asked to wait while Elsie Brody took the recording and typed up Terry's declaration. Twenty minutes later, she brought the papers back, Terry signed the declaration, and Chief Durham witnessed his signature.

Before leaving, Terry gave Jim his address, phone numbers, cell, home, and work. Jim said he or the District Attorney's office would be in touch. He told Terry when the case went to trial that he would be called as the principal witness for the prosecution.

After Terry had gone, the three men stayed seated behind a closed door.

The chief said, "This is quite an unexpected development, Jim. After all these years, Terry Wells finally gives his version of what happened to Doreen Warren on the night of her tragic death. Do you think he's telling the truth, Jim?"

"Yes, Chief, I do. There's no reason for him to lie."

"Why do you think he waited so long to tell the story of what he witnessed that night?" Tony asked.

"I think when he met Buck Woods a week or so ago at the Home Depot, where he works, they talked about that night, and he could see how distressed Buck was after all this time. I guess the guilt ate away at him, and he decided to tell the truth. I'm sure his fear of Rusty had something to do with Terry not coming forward sooner."

"Well, now that Terry has come forward and given his declaration, we don't have a choice. We'll have to issue a warrant to arrest Brenda for second-degree murder and Rusty on obstruction of justice and intimidation of a witness," the chief said.

"As if Rusty and Brenda don't have enough problems, this will be devastating for their children," Tony said.

"It's not pleasant for any of us," Jim said.

"Before we go ahead with the arrest warrants, I think we should contact Judge Parker and ask her to issue a search warrant for their house, outbuildings, and vehicles," the chief said.

"What reason can we give for the warrant?" Tony asked.

"I can think of a few reasons. We're still looking for the .38 caliber pistol used in the Wayne Blackmore murder. Brenda Sykes is a suspect in that case, and the records show she owned a .38 caliber handgun. Terry Wells said he saw her snatch the locket from Doreen Warren's neck the night of her death. For some unknown reason, she may have kept it—two good reasons to issue a search warrant, don't you think?"

"Would you like me to take care of getting the warrants issued, Chief?" Jim asked.

"I think we can let Tony take care of that, Jim. After all, he did volunteer to assist you."

"No problem, Chief," Tony said, "I'll get right on it."

"Okay, gentlemen, that's it for now."

When Jim got home that evening, he updated Buck and Shawna on what had happened at the police station. They weren't surprised to hear about the arrest and search warrants now that Terry Wells had come forward with his eyewitness account.

"Jim, I brought you a present."

"What kind of present?"

"I'll go get it. It's in my truck."

Buck left and returned with a clear plastic trash bag a few minutes later. It held an old corn broom and a black plastic dustpan.

"I went to look for firewood behind the storage shed and found the broom and dustpan under a pile of leaves. It looked like someone had tried to hide them. I remembered that someone had swept the floor. I had my work gloves on, so if there are any fingerprints on the broom handle or dustpan, they should still be there."

"Thanks, Buck. I'll have them checked out to see if any prints come up. Maybe this is the break we need. Whoever swept the floor in the cabin didn't want to leave any shoe prints—maybe they left fingerprints. I'll send them over to the crime lab in the morning."

CHAPTER 21

The next morning, Jim showed the chief the possible new evidence Buck had found. He took the bag from Jim and assigned an officer to drive the items to the crime lab.

As Jim was about to leave the chief's office, Tony Timpano stopped by and said, "I've got the arrest and search warrants. We're ready to roll."

The chief said, "That's good news, Tony. Did you have any problems convincing Judge Parker?"

"She was a little hesitant initially, but after I explained the whole story, it didn't take long for her to agree and sign the papers."

"By the way," Chief Durham said, "I called assistant DA Paul Prentice and explained what's happening. He'll be dropping by later this morning to go over the evidence. It's time to get it done, Captain. Take Jim and Officers Walker and Talbot. They should be in the patrol room having a coffee. Tell them to follow you in their cruiser."

"Okay, Chief, we're on our way."

Tony rang the bell, and Brenda appeared at the door a few minutes later. She looked dumbfounded when she saw four police officers standing on the front porch.

"Good morning, Brenda." Captain Timpano showed her the arrest warrant and said, "Brenda Jane Sykes, I have the unpleasant duty of informing you that you are under arrest for second-degree murder in the death of Doreen Patricia Warren on the night of Saturday, June 25th, 1988."

Tony continued, "I would like to inform you of your rights. You have the right to remain silent. Anything you say can and will be used against you in court. You have the right to an attorney and have him present while being questioned. If you cannot afford to hire an attorney, one will be appointed to represent you free of charge before questioning if you wish. If you decide to make a statement, you may stop anytime. Do you understand each of these rights? Having these rights in mind, do you wish to talk to us now?"

Brenda's face turned ashen gray. She broke down, tears flooding her face. Weakly, she said, "Yes. I understand my rights and choose not to talk until my lawyer is present."

Brenda looked like she was about to collapse. Jim reached out and grabbed her arm to help steady her.

Tony continued, "We have a search warrant for your house, garage, outbuildings, and vehicles. The warrant specifically states we are searching for a .38 caliber pistol as a possible murder weapon in the death of Wayne Daniel Blackmore. The search warrant also specifies a gold locket belonging to Doreen Patricia Warren."

When Tony had finished, Jim stepped in and asked Brenda to place her hands behind her back. He cuffed Brenda and ushered her out the front door, where Officer Craig Walker took her by the arm and led her to the waiting cruiser.

Just as Craig placed Brenda into the backseat, Rusty charged down the hallway like a mad bull in a china shop and yelled, "What the hell's goin' on here? Where are you takin', Brenda?"

Tony intercepted him and said, "Calm down, Rusty, and I'll explain if you'll be quiet for a minute."

He told Rusty that Brenda was being arrested for second-degree murder in the death of Doreen Patricia Warren and the reasons for the search warrant.

Rusty screamed, "No fuckin' way you're searchin' my property."

Rusty went berserk. He took a wild swing at Tony, who ducked just in time. While he was off-balance, Capino hit him with a left uppercut that stunned Rusty long enough for Jim and Mark Talbot to rush over and subdue him. While Mark held his hands behind his back, Jim slapped handcuffs onto his wrists. They led Rusty into the kitchen, sat him on a chair, and told him to shut his mouth.

Captain Timpano produced the arrest warrant and said, "Russell

Donald Sykes, you are under arrest for obstruction of justice and intimidating a witness in the murder of Doreen Patrica Warren." Tony read him his rights.

Officer Talbot grabbed Rusty's arm, stood him up, marched him out the front door to the police cruiser, and sat him next to Brenda. Then Officer Talbot slid into the shotgun seat, and Officer Walker started the engine and drove off headed for Bangor and the Penobscot County Jail.

The kitchen was a mess. Unwashed dishes filled the sink, and the table contained a silver metal ashtray overflowing with what appeared to be cannabis butts. Recently, Rusty's doctor approved medicinal marijuana to help alleviate severe back pain caused by a herniated disc.

The search was still underway when officers Talbot and Walker returned from Bangor. So far, they had gone through the main floor without finding anything. The officers were assigned to search the garage and vehicles while Jim and Tony checked the upper level of the house.

As Jim searched Brenda's jewel box, he almost missed it. The bottom of the red felt lining had a small slit about an inch long. It looked like a sharp knife, or a razor blade might have cut it. He poked his baby finger inside and felt a hard object. Jim pulled a penknife from his pocket, shoving the blade into the slit in the jewel box. It took him a few minutes of fishing, but he finally snagged the chain and slid it out. To his amazement, he was staring at a heart-shaped locket with a broken chain. The inscription read, "To Doreen, love, Buck."

"Tony." Jim yelled, his heart pounding, "Get in here. Guess what I just found?"

"What is it?" Tony asked as he came rushing into the room.

"Look." Jim held up Doreen's necklace. "Just like Terry said."

"Wow," Tony gasped. "It looks like we've got the proof we need. Bag and label it, Jim."

After searching the rest of the house, including the basement, no gun turned up.

Tony and Jim decided to join Craig and Mark to see how they were doing. They had checked the garage and two cars without finding anything. The last place left to search was the storage shed. While the other three were double-checking the garage and vehicles, Jim went into the shed. After doing what he thought was a thorough search, he was about to give up when he spotted a pile of oily rags next to an old gas-powered lawn mower. Jim kicked the rags aside and found a wooden cigar box. It was large enough to hold a pistol. Excited, Jim wondered what he'd find. To his surprise, the box was empty when he flipped up the lid.

CHAPTER 22

Kaleb Swartz, a criminal lawyer, was sixty years old, short in stature, a little overweight, and his hair had waved him goodbye a long time ago. With his dark-rimmed glasses, he looked like he could pass as the twin brother of movie actor Danny DeVito. Kaleb was a senior partner in the local law firm of Swartz, Steinberg & Goldstein. Like a shark sensing blood, Kaleb waited patiently in his car in the parking lot behind the Orono Police Department. When he saw two police officers return, he bounded out of his vehicle and, running as fast as his short legs would allow, followed them through the back entrance before the door locked automatically.

Chief Durham was in the middle of a conversation with ADA Paul Prentice when Swartz came charging in like a bull in a china shop and began to shout. "I just received a phone call from my clients, Rusty and Brenda Sykes. What the hell are they doing in the Penobscot County Jail? Would you like to explain what's going on here? What's this cock-and-bull story about Brenda being arrested on a murder charge and Rusty for intimidating a witness and obstruction of justice?"

"Mr. Swartz, please cool down! Come in, and let's discuss this calmly."

Swartz took a chair and said, "I don't want your officers questioning my clients without my presence."

With a half-smile, Paul Prentice said, "Hello, Kaleb. Nice to see you again."

Swartz nodded without speaking and turned back to the chief, but before he could open his mouth, Chief Durham glared at him and, in a scolding tone, said, "Now, Kaleb, you know better than that. You can go to the Penobscot County Jail and speak with Brenda and Rusty privately, and we won't do any interviewing unless you are present."

By this time, Swartz had calmed down. His grandstanding act over, he got to his feet and said, "I'll head over there now." Without another word, he left.

Brenda Sykes sat on a wooden bench in a holding cell at the Penobscot County Jail, bent over with her head in her hands, softly crying. Rusty sat on the opposite bench, scowling. His reddish-orange hair was greasy and unwashed, and his cheeks were on fire from his spiked blood pressure.

When Kaleb entered, Brenda lifted her head, wiped her eyes with the back of her hand, and in a weak, child-like voice said, "Thank God you're here, Mr. Swartz."

Kaleb ignored Rusty, sat down next to Brenda, put his hand on her shoulder, and said, "Brenda, my dear, please take your time and tell me what this is about."

After Brenda told him she was charged with second-degree murder in Doreen Warren's death in 1988, Kaleb asked, "How old were you at the time?"

"I was seventeen," she whispered.

"What evidence have they come up with after all these years?"

"They said an eyewitness came forward and gave them a statement. He said he saw me arguing with Doreen Warren, rip off her necklace, pick up a rock, and hit her on the forehead—and after I struck her, Doreen fell into the river."

"Is that what happened?"

"Yes. It was long ago, and I was drunk that night and didn't mean to hurt her. We were arguing, and I got angry and reacted without thinking. I've regretted it all my life and will until the day I die. I still have bad dreams about that horrible night."

"Who is this eyewitness, do you know?"

"Yes, his name is Terry Wells."

"I'm wondering why it took him all these years to come forward."

"Rusty was also there at the time. He threatened Terry and told him not to tell anyone, especially the police, what he had witnessed. He told Terry he would be dead meat if he breathed a word to a single person. Terry was always afraid of Rusty, and he believed him and was too frightened to tell anyone until now."

"Well, we've got a bit of a dilemma. I think second-degree murder is too harsh. Since you were so young, maybe we can work out a plea bargain and get the charges reduced to manslaughter. You may get five to ten years, but with good behavior, you could be out in three to five years, depending on the length of the sentence. If we plead not guilty to the current charge, if convicted, you could receive a sentence of twenty-five to thirty years without the possibility of parole for at least ten to fifteen years. You'll have to decide if you want to go to trial and take your chances or if you wish to plead guilty to manslaughter instead. A long, drawn-out trial could be costly, and I can't guarantee a favorable outcome. Now that an eyewitness has come forward, your odds of beating the second-degree murder charge won't be good."

Brenda sobbed, "I just want this nightmare to go away."

Rusty was still fuming when Kaleb went over and sat next to him. Kaleb repeated Brenda's story, and Rusty confirmed what Brenda had said was accurate.

Kaleb motioned for Brenda to come and join them. "Well," he said, "you two have got yourselves into a fine pickle. I think we can get Brenda's charge reduced to manslaughter. I'm going to try for involuntary manslaughter. As far as you're concerned, Rusty, I'm unsure what we can do. We can say it's his word against yours because Brenda witnessed your threat. If Brenda takes the stand and lies under oath, and they find out, she will be charged with perjury. We don't have a lot of options here. I'll talk to the prosecuting attorney, whom I believe will be Assistant DA Paul Prentice, and see if we can work out a plea bargain. I'll work on it and get back to you soon."

Kaleb signaled to the guard and took his leave. When he arrived back in Orono, he parked his car in the back lot, ran to the front of the building, and bolted up the stairs. He flew past Elsie Brody and headed down the stairs.

Elsie yelled, "Mr. Swartz, you can't go down there unannounced. The door is locked, and you won't get in."

Kaleb ignored her and kept on going. When he got to the door, he yelled and pounded until Chief Durham came and opened it. He barged past the chief and into his office, where Paul Prentice sat reading papers.

On his heels, the chief barked, "What the hell's going on, Kaleb?"

Swartz ignored the chief, and, looking at Paul Prentice, panting and out of breath, he said, "I'm glad you're still here, Paul. We need to talk."

The Assistant DA looked perturbed. He asked, "What's it regarding, Kaleb?"

Kaleb began to rattle on. "Paul, I think the charge of second-degree murder under the circumstances is way too harsh. Brenda was only seventeen at the time. She was under the age of majority and would have been tried as a juvenile. There's no proof that the blow to her head killed Doreen Warren. She could have only been stunned and died from drowning. In the heat of an argument under the influence of alcohol, Brenda acted impulsively with no intent to commit murder. In my eyes, Doreen Warren's death was an unfortunate accident. However, after discussing it with my client, we would be willing to plead guilty to a charge of involuntary manslaughter. Eliminating a trial will save the state and my client a lot of expense. If you stick with the second-degree murder charge, we will fight it in court. Concerning Rusty, the charge of obstruction of justice and intimidating a witness is also much too harsh. Rusty was a juvenile at the time as well. He was trying to be a knight in shining armor and protect his girlfriend. Perhaps you could consider that and recommend a fine without jail time. I think the obstruction charge should be dropped entirely. At the time, he could have pled the fifth. If they are both sentenced to serve time in prison, there won't be anyone left to look after their two teenage children."

After hearing Kaleb out, Prentice took a deep breath and exhaled slowly. "I will discuss your offer with my boss, District Attorney Richard Whales, later today and let you know his decision as soon as possible."

"Here's my card. Please call my cell number. I look forward to hearing from you later this evening." Kaleb turned and abruptly left the room.

Feeling like a tornado had touched down in his office, Chief Durham looked at Prentice, smiled, and shrugged.

CHAPTER 23

I t was getting late, and Jim felt mentally and physically exhausted.
When his phone rang, he was about to head home for dinner
and a drink.

"Detective Barkowsky," he answered.

"Hi, Jim. I'm glad I caught you," Paul Prentice said.

"Hey, Paul, what's up?"

"I discussed the Doreen Warren case with my boss, Richard
Whales, and have decided to accept a plea bargain to the lesser
charge of voluntary manslaughter. I called Kaleb and let him know
our decision. He was pushing for involuntary manslaughter. I told
him that was our best and final offer—take it or leave it. When he
realized we wouldn't budge, he decided to accept. I could sense he
was reluctant to go to court on the second-degree murder charge.
You won't need to question Brenda or Rusty now that we have the
tentative plea bargain agreement. Brenda is to appear before a
magistrate day after tomorrow for her arraignment. We'll change
the charge, and she'll plead guilty to voluntary manslaughter. After
considering all the evidence, the judge will schedule a date for
sentencing. I would appreciate your informing Captain Timpano
and Chief Durham of the plea bargain. As far as Rusty is concerned,
we have decided to drop the obstruction of justice charge. However,
the intimidating a witness charge still stands. I believe he's scheduled
for his arraignment and bail hearing the day after tomorrow. The
obstruction of justice charge is not as relevant now that Brenda has
pleaded guilty to the manslaughter charge. Should Rusty plead guilty
to the intimidating a witness charge, we'll recommend a substantial
fine instead of jail time, so Rusty will be home to look after their two

children." He laughed. "Believe it or not, even prosecutors have a heart."

"Thanks, Paul. The chief and Tony have already checked out for the night. I'll inform them first thing tomorrow morning."

"Okay, thanks, Jim. Talk to you soon."

By the time Jim got home, everyone had eaten, and Shawna had left his roast beef dinner on a plate in the refrigerator.

He popped the plate into the microwave and nuked it for three minutes. He retrieved a beer from the refrigerator, then joined Buck and Shawna in the family room. Sipping red wine, they were anxious to hear about his day.

As he sat wolfing down his food and sipping on his beer, Jim related the story of the arrest of Brenda and Rusty. He told them about Rusty's scuffle with Tony and saved the best for last—finding Doreen's locket hidden in Brenda's jewel box.

After Jim had finished his story, Buck said, "I'm surprised Brenda kept the locket all these years. That piece of incriminating evidence proves Terry told the truth."

"I can't believe she kept the locket either," Shawna said. That was dumb of her."

Jim went on to tell them about the plea bargain and that Brenda would plead guilty to voluntary manslaughter rather than go to trial on the second-degree murder charge. He told them about what Paul Prentice had said about Rusty's charges. They were glad to hear that he may be around to look after their children.

As tears glistened in Buck's eyes, he said, "Well, at least Doreen's death will finally have some closure. Is someone going to inform her parents?"

"Yes. It looks like that will be my job," Jim said.

Shawna asked, "What do you think Brenda's sentence will be?"

"My best guess is eight to ten years. With good behavior, Brenda could be out in four to six years. It will all depend on how the judge views the case. Because she was a juvenile when the death occurred, he'll probably consider that when making his decision. We'll have to wait and see."

"What about the Wayne Blackmore case? Any more progress?" Buck asked.

"Not at the moment. I'll have to devote more time to it starting tomorrow. I think there are some things that Donna Blackmore isn't telling me, and I may have to go and see her again." Jim said.

"What about the bag I found at the cabin—any word from the crime lab?"

"Not yet. I thought I would've heard something by now. It slipped my mind with all that's been happening with Rusty and Brenda."

"By the way," Shawna asked, "how are things coming along at the cabin, Buck?"

"Things are going great! I've installed all the new flooring and fixed the front porch. I bought and installed a new front door. As you know, the roof was re-shingled, and now that the flooring is finished, I'm getting ready to install the new bathroom fixtures and kitchen sink. I've hired a neighbor to help install the kitchen cabinets. When the new appliances are installed, that should be it. The last thing to do is shop for new furniture for the kitchen, living room, and bedrooms. I can finally put my feet up and relax when that's done. Maybe even do a little fishing."

"Sounds like things are taking shape," Jim said. "Wish I had more time to give you a hand."

"No problem, Telly. The best thing you can do is catch Wayne Blackmore's killer."

"Don't I wish," Jim said as he stretched and yawned.

CHAPTER 24

Jim called Donna Blackmore first thing Monday morning. The phone rang and rang. On the fifth ring, she answered.

"Hello," she said, out of breath.

"Good morning, Donna. It's Detective Jim Barkowsky," he said cheerily.

"Detective Barkowsky, I'm surprised to hear from you. To what do I owe the pleasure? Are you making any progress in Wayne's murder investigation? I hope you've got some good news?"

"I wish I had some good news. We still haven't found the murder weapon,"

"That's too bad. I hope you find it soon."

"When we last talked, I could sense you were holding something back, and you seemed frightened. Does it have anything to do with the Catalini brothers?"

Donna paused momentarily, and Jim could hear her taking a deep breath. Finally, she began to sob and whispered, "As you know, those damn gangsters came to Wayne's funeral service. They told me Wayne owed them one hundred thousand dollars plus interest for a gambling debt. Since Wayne was dead, they expected me to honor his debt and pay it in full with interest of four hundred thousand dollars within one week. They wanted me to deposit five hundred thousand dollars into an offshore Cayman Islands bank account. When I told them I didn't have that kind of cash, they hinted my boys and I might have an accident. I was terrified! That's when I told them about the insurance money. Somehow, I believe they already knew about the two million dollars. I think they were testing me. I suspect they must have told Wayne they would kill his family if he didn't come up with the money. That's when I guess he must have told them about the life insurance. I think they had the idea to kill him and collect from me once I received the settlement. Wayne tried to protect us by sacrificing his life for us. Joe Catalini told me not to contact the police or else. I got the message. They didn't say it, but I'm sure they planned to kill my boys and me if I didn't pay up. I'm so scared, and I don't know what to do. If they find out, I told you, they would kill us. I hope you will protect us and bring those crooks to justice."

For a minute, Jim lost his tongue. When he gathered his thoughts, he said, "Donna, I'm glad you told me. Yes, we will protect you and your boys. There's no way they will find out, you told me. Have you received the insurance settlement yet?"

"I expect I will be receiving it today or tomorrow."

"Okay, here's what I'd like you to do. Carry on as normally as possible. Are you to contact the brothers when the money is received and transferred into the bank account number they gave you?"

"Yes, they left me a phone number to call when I received the money, and the deposit was completed."

"What do you think will happen if you don't comply with their instructions?"

"I think they will try to kill us."

"We're not going to let that happen. Here's what we're going to do." Jim outlined his plan.

In a shaky voice, Donna asked, "If I go along with your plan, how will you protect us?"

"I'll personally stay with you and the boys. We'll set up police surveillance to watch your property around the clock. I guarantee we'll keep you safe."

"When will this happen?"

"We'll start immediately. Based on what you said earlier, the money could arrive today or tomorrow, and we don't have much time to get the ball rolling. We'll formulate a plan to obtain the needed evidence when I get there. I'll see you mid-afternoon, and I'll come prepared to stay for a few days if necessary."

"No problem, Detective. We have plenty of room. See you soon!"

When Jim hung up, he sat at his desk, his head spinning. After his thoughts were in order, he took a couple of deep breaths, then headed down the hallway. Jim stopped at Tony Timpano's office and asked Tony to join him for a meeting with the chief. Without asking why he got up and followed Jim into the chief's office.

"To what do I owe the pleasure of your company, gentlemen?"

"You're not going to believe this, Chief."

He told them about his conversation with Donna Blackmore and his plan.

"This could be the break in the Blackmore case we've been waiting for."

"I agree," Tony said.

"Jim, why don't you call Buck and see if he'd be willing to help? It might be better if you stay with the Blackmore family to ensure their protection, and Tony can work out of the office and help coordinate things."

"Okay, Chief. I'll give Buck a call."

Buck agreed to help. At two o'clock, they met at the house and packed. Jim called Shawana to inform her of what was happening before leaving for the Blackmore residence. The wheels were in motion!

CHAPTER 25

They arrived at the Blackmore residence at two forty-five, and as they exited Jim's car, a car pulled in behind them.

Andy Graves, a young officer who had been on the force for about four years, was a computer geek, and his expertise had come in handy on several occasions. Dressed in his police uniform, he carried a small black case that contained the equipment to carry out Jim's plan. Andy's round blue eyes lit up when he saw the two men.

"Hi, Andy," Jim said, "I'd like you to meet homicide Detective Buck Woods. Buck is a good friend who's on vacation from the NYPD. The chief has approved, and Buck has agreed to help solve the Wayne Blackmore murder case."

The two men shook hands and followed Jim to the front door. Jim rang the bell, and in a few minutes, Donna Blackmore greeted them with a relieved smile. "Welcome, gentlemen." Donna had spent some time preening in front of a mirror and looked stunning. As they stepped into the foyer, the sweet fragrance of her perfume filled the air.

Jim introduced Buck and Andy, and they followed her down the hallway to the family room. After the men were seated, Donna excused herself. A few minutes later, Donna returned carrying a silver tray with four mugs of coffee, cream, and sugar. She set the tray on the coffee table and left the room again. In a few minutes, she returned carrying a plate.

"I almost forgot. I baked oatmeal cookies this morning," Donna said, placing the plate on the coffee table. "Sorry, I didn't have time to go out and buy doughnuts."

They all laughed at her little jab.

"I hope you don't mind, Donna. Buck is a close friend who is a vacationing homicide detective with the New York Police Department. With Chief Durham's approval, Buck has volunteered to help. He's been assigned to work with me on the case and to keep you and your boys safe. Buck owns the cabin where your husband's body was discovered," Jim said.

"Not a great way to be spending your vacation, Detective. However, I appreciate you taking the time to help detective Barkowsky, and it will make me feel safer with two detectives in the house."

"Mrs. Blackmore, I hope my years of NYPD experience will help Detective Barkowsky catch your husband's killer."

"Thank you, Detective. I won't rest easy until Wayne's murder is solved. By the way, please call me Donna."

"Okay, Donna, it is," Buck said.

"I'm curious," Jim asked, "where are Bobby and Billy?"

"I asked my sister, Beth, if they could stay with her for a few nights. I told a little white lie and said I had to go out of town for a few days."

"Where does your sister live?" Buck asked.

"She and her husband Carl live a few miles from here."

"They'll probably be safe there," Jim said, "but I don't want to take any chances. Please give me their address, and I'll arrange a cruiser to watch your sister's house until this is over."

After Donna provided Jim with her sister's address, he called Chief Durham on his cell phone, explained the situation, and gave him the address. The chief said they were a little short-staffed, but he would call his counterpart in Bangor and have him look after it. Jim thanked the chief and hung up.

"Thanks, Detective. I feel much better knowing they will be protected."

"I doubt the Catalini brothers would know the boys' whereabouts, but as I said, I don't want to take any chances," Jim said.

"Where do you want me to set up?" Andy asked.

"I think the office would be the best room. Is that okay with you, Donna?" Jim said.

"Yes, that's fine. It's the best place."

"Let's go take a look," Andy suggested.

They excused themselves and headed to the office.

"This looks great," Andy said. "I'll get started, and it won't take long."

They left Andy to do his thing, and Jim and Buck returned to the family room to discuss their plan with Donna.

When they were seated, Jim said, "Buck and I have devised a plan of action, so you'll know what you'll say when you contact the Catalini brothers." He outlined their plan, and Donna agreed.

Andy finished his work by four, returned to the family room, and asked Jim and Buck to join him in the office.

"The recorder we are using is the latest technology. It has a built-in CD-RW drive, and the CD-R holds over 300 hours of recordings. It stores 15,000 calls on one CD. The software that comes with it allows the information to be transferred to a computer. The recorder will start as soon as you pick up the phone, and outgoing calls will start as soon as the other party picks up." He reviewed the features and left a manual in case they needed it.

"Looks simple enough," Buck said. "Thanks, Andy, great job!"

"If there aren't any questions, I'll be on my way."

"Nothing I can think of," Jim said.

"Nothing I can think of, either," Buck said.

After shaking hands with Jim and Buck, on his way out, Andy stopped by the family room, said goodbye, and thanked Donna for her hospitality.

Jim awoke to a noise that sounded like a hundred tiny elves tap dancing on the roof. As his head cleared, he realized he was at Donna Blackmore's house in one of the guest bedrooms. The roaring wind and rain wildly beating against the bedroom window sent a chill down his spine. The weather forecast had called for a nor'easter, and it appeared to be right on schedule.

By eight, Jim and Buck were showered and dressed. Donna was

frying bacon, scrambling eggs, and making toast as they entered the kitchen. Everything smelled scrumptious.

Donna smiled and said, "Good morning, gentlemen. I trust you both slept well,"

"Like a baby," Jim said.

"Like a rock," Buck said.

"Breakfast will be ready shortly. I hope you like bacon, scrambled eggs, and toast. There's fresh-squeezed orange juice in the fridge, and the coffee's ready. Help yourself."

"You didn't have to go to all this trouble," Jim said, "but we certainly appreciate it."

"Thanks. Everything smells so good!" Buck said.

"We've got quite a storm today," Donna said, glancing out the kitchen window.

"By the sound of the wind and rain, it's a good day to stay inside where it's warm and dry," Jim said.

"Amen to that, brother," Buck said.

After enjoying the great breakfast, the men insisted on cleaning up. They told Donna to take her coffee and relax in the family room. Ten minutes later, they joined Donna carrying a second cup of coffee. The doorbell chimed just as they sat down, and everyone looked puzzled.

"Who could be out on such a nasty day?" Buck paused for a second. "I bet it's the good ole postal service."

"Maybe it's the mailman with your check, Donna," Jim said.

"You could be right, Detective."

Donna excused herself, got up, and headed to the front door. Buck and Jim could hear her carrying on a muted conversation with what sounded like a male voice. When she returned, Donna was beaming.

"You were right, Detective Woods. It was the postal service." She opened the envelope and removed a certified check from Global World Insurance, Inc. for two million dollars.

"Well," Jim said, "it's time we put our plan into action."

When they were in the office, Jim went over the script with Donna, and in a few minutes, she was ready.

Jim and Buck put on headphones and nodded to Donna. She dialed the number. After three rings, a gruff male voice answered.

"Hello."

"This is Donna Blackmore. Who am I speaking to?"

"This is Joe Catalini. I hope you're calling with good news, Mrs. Blackmore."

"Yes and no," Donna said, trying to remain calm.

"This is Carmen Catalini. What do you mean by that, Mrs. Blackmore?"

It was apparent they had put the call on speakerphone.

"The good news is I received the check this morning. The bad news is that I have reconsidered the amount I will deposit into the account number you gave me."

Agitated, Joe said, "What do you mean you've reconsidered? There's no negotiating the amount. Deposit five hundred thousand dollars or else, Mrs. Blackmore."

"The amount you requested to settle my late husband's debt is unreasonable. For a debt of one hundred thousand, you want five hundred thousand, four hundred thousand in interest—that's outrageous. I'm only paying you one hundred and fifty thousand, not one penny more. Even that's too much!"

"Look here, Mrs. Blackmore," Carmen shouted, "you're in no position to bargain. You're lucky we didn't ask for one million or even the whole two million. If you don't pay us the five hundred thousand, you and your family will end up the same way we took care of your husband—dead."

"That's right, Mrs. Blackmore," Joe said. "Don't play games with us. You have forty-eight hours to transfer the five hundred thousand into the offshore account number we provided, and don't call the cops. If you do, you and your boys will be killed."

Click!

As Donna hung up the phone, her legs felt like rubber, and her stomach was nauseous, but she had never felt so relieved in all her life.

"Bingo!" Jim said.

Jim and Buck gave each other a high-five, smiling like two Cheshire cats. They had the evidence to charge the Catalini brothers with loan sharking, extortion, and murder.

"Great work, Donna! Thanks to you, we've got the evidence to charge the Catalini brothers with loan sharking, extortion, and murder," Buck said, smiling.

"We got them," Jim grinned.

As a precaution, Buck stayed with Donna while Jim rushed the recording back to the Orono Police Station.

Jim downloaded the conversation onto his computer at the office and recorded it to a CD. He asked Captain Timpano to join him in Chief Durham's office. When Jim played the conversation, Chief Durham and Captain Timpano were pleased.

"Good work, Jim! Send a copy of the recording to Chief O'Brien at the Boston PD and tell him to call me after he has listened to it," the chief said.

Twenty minutes after Jim had sent the recording to the Boston PD, Chief Durham's phone rang. It was Chief O'Brien.

When he had hung up, Chief Durham went to Jim's office, smiled, and said, "Great work, Jim. Based on the evidence you and Buck gathered, the Boston PD is issuing arrest warrants for the Catalini brothers for murder, loan sharking, and extortion. They'll let us know as soon as they have them in custody. Since we know who killed Wayne Blackmore, you can call off the gun registration search. Even though we still don't have the gun, we've got enough evidence. It looks like the murder weapon won't be needed. If it turns up, it will be a bonus."

An hour later, Chief Durham's phone rang.

"Chief Durham."

"It's Chief O'Brien. I've got good news. The Catalini brothers were arrested without incident and are in the Boston City Jail. Tomorrow they will be delivered to the Penobscot County Jail in Bangor, the jurisdiction where the murder occurred. An arraignment and a bail hearing will be scheduled within forty-eight hours. The evidence Detective Barkowsky collected should send them away for life."

"That's excellent news, Chief. Thanks, and have a good day."

Jim was ecstatic when the chief told him about the arrest of the Catalini brothers. He called Donna and Buck to relay the good news, saying Buck could come home now that the threat to Donna and her boys was over!

CHAPTER 26

Joe and Carmen Catalini stared at one another through the bars of adjoining cells. They stood as close as they could and carried on a whispered conversation.

"How could we have been so stupid," Carmen grumbled. "I never suspected for one minute that conniving bitch would go to the police."

"Yeah," Joe said, "I could've sworn that she was so scared of what we said we'd do to her and her kids that she wouldn't dare involve the cops. Boy, did we screw up!"

"Our lawyer should be here any minute. He'll be pissed off to find out that our conversation with that bitch was recorded. We'll tell him we didn't do it, and we're going to plead not guilty," Carmen whispered.

"There's no way they'll ever believe us when we plead not guilty. I'd rather not go to trial," Joe said. "With that recording, we don't stand a chance. We've got to figure out how to get out of here. I don't think any judge in his right mind would grant us bail based on the charges and our record."

"I'm guessing we'll be sent to a jail in Bangor. Once we know the date, we can make arrangements with the boys," Carmen said.

"Our lawyer should be able to find out when that's going to happen, and we can set something up with Mario," Joe responded.

"I don't think they're gonna question us here," Carmen said. "I bet that'll happen when we get to Bangor."

"We won't have to worry about that if we don't get there," Joe chuckled.

Carmen grinned and said, "Then let's ensure we don't get there."

Looking between the bars, they spotted a police officer accompanying their smartly dressed lawyer down the hallway.

Their lawyer informed them that since the alleged crime had occurred in Penobscot County, they would be transferred from the Boston City Jail to the Penobscot County Jail in Bangor for their arraignment and bail hearing.

At two o'clock the day after their arrest, the two brothers, wearing orange prison uniforms, handcuffs, and leg irons, were loaded into the back of a black SUV for the 240-mile drive to Bangor.

A short distance from the jail, as the SUV turned onto Sudbury Street, a white cargo van came out of nowhere, slamming into the front driver-side fender.

"What the hell," the officer behind the wheel yelled as he jammed on the brakes.

The driver of the van stayed behind the wheel. Two men wearing black ski masks jumped out carrying UZI semi-automatic pistols and attacked the SUV. They fired several rounds directly through the windows, killing both police officers before they could draw their weapons.

One of the masked men grabbed the keys to the cuffs and shackles from the dead driver's belt. They dragged the Catalini brothers out of the SUV and tossed them into the van. The driver punched the accelerator, and the van squealed away, leaving smoking black rubber marks on the pavement. The whole operation took less than thirty seconds.

A few pedestrians and one person in a passing car witnessed the murder, and they described the getaway van to the first police officers on the scene. A BOLO was issued immediately upon obtaining the description of the vehicle.

An hour later, the Boston police found the abandoned van on a gravel road outside the city. Earlier that morning, the vehicle was stolen from a parking garage in downtown Boston, and the van had been wiped clean—a professional job from start to finish.

After their escape, a nationwide search began. Chief O'Brien rounded up every snitch and underworld informant in the Boston area. Detectives grilled them relentlessly for hours without success. It was as if the Catalini brothers had vanished from the face of the earth. A few days went by without any clues as to their whereabouts. Rumor had it that they had somehow slipped through the dragnet, had gotten out of the country, and were hiding in Mexico or South America.

Two hours after the SUV had been attacked and the Catalini brothers had escaped, Jim and Captain Tony Timpano met with Chief Durham in his office. With a grim face, the chief said, "Gentlemen, I just received some bad news from Chief O'Brien. Earlier this afternoon, the Catalini brothers' vehicle was attacked shortly after leaving for Bangor. The two police officers were massacred in cold blood, and three unknown suspects grabbed the brothers and escaped in a stolen van. Not long after their escape, police found the vehicle abandoned on a county road outside Boston. After checking the vehicle, no fingerprints or other evidence was found to help identify the killers."

For a moment, Tony and Jim sat in shocked silence, trying to process the information.

Finally, Jim said, "Chief, I can't believe what I just heard. How the hell could it happen? Two police officers are dead, and the Catalini brothers are in the wind. It all seems like a bad dream."

"Believe it, Jim," the chief said. "It looks like the Boston PD underestimated the reach of those two slime balls. The Morano crime family is suspected of planning and carrying out the carjacking, but proving it will be hard. All lips appear to be sealed. So far, police informants have proven to be useless, and no one is talking."

Tony spoke up. "I'm concerned for the safety of Mrs. Blackmore and her two boys. The Catalini brothers may be out for revenge now that they're on the lam, knowing that Donna Blackmore got the police involved."

"Good point, Captain. I think it might be wise to post a squad car to watch her house just in case they try something," Jim said.

"Good idea, Jim. I'll call Chief James in Bangor, explain the situation, and have him place a watch on her house immediately."

"I'll call Donna Blackmore," Jim said, "and let her know what happened and inform her of the police protection, so she won't be alarmed when a patrol car shows up on her doorstep."

CHAPTER 27

After abandoning the stolen van, the Catalini brothers got into an inconspicuous blue Honda Civic sedan. They changed clothes on the fly, throwing their prison uniforms out of the moving vehicle. When they arrived at a predetermined spot on the Charles River, a beautifully restored Norseman C-64 pontoon plane owned and flown by their nephew, Mario Morano, awaited their arrival. In less than five minutes, the plane took off, and Carmen and Joe gazed down at the sprawling city of Boston—free men.

At thirty-four years of age, Mario Morano was the middle son of the three sons of Maria and Santino Morano. Maria, the older sister of Joe and Carmen Catalini, had married the current Boston mob boss when she turned twenty-one. Back then, Santino Morano, an ambitious young man, started as an associate and gradually worked up to his present position as street boss.

Joe spoke into his headset microphone to Mario, "Man, this is some airplane, but it's noisy. How old is it?"

"Yeah, it's noisy. That's why we need noise-reduction headsets to talk. To answer your question, I think it was built in the forties," Mario replied. "I bought it five years ago from a collector, completely restored. When my dad and the boys want to get away for a meeting, I fly them to the five-bedroom cabin where I'm taking you. The cabin is more like a hunting and fishing lodge that my dad uses several times yearly. It's peaceful and a good place to do business without interruptions. Since the plane has ten seats, everyone has plenty of room. Sometimes I fly my mom, two brothers, and dad to the cabin for a vacation. My dad believes in spending quality time with his family."

Carmen was listening in on the conversation, and he asked, "Where was the plane built?"

"Believe it or not, it was built in Canada by Noorduyn. For many years, Norseman planes have been the workhorses of the Canadian north."

"No shit," Joe said.

Cruising at 134 knots, it took a little under two hours to reach their destination. Mario landed perfectly on the glass-like surface of the small lake in northern Maine. He taxied up to the sturdy wooden dock that extended forty feet into the lake. When the plane was secured, the gear and his two uncles unloaded, Mario gave them a quick rundown on operating the gas generator. After Mario started the generator, he said, "There's enough fuel to last about three weeks. I'll come back in two weeks with more fuel and supplies." He said goodbye and headed toward the plane. The engine roared to life a few minutes later as the airplane lifted off and disappeared into an overcast sky.

A week later, as he peered out the living room window overlooking the lake, Carmen said, "I'm going stir-crazy."

"Yeah, me too. I'm a city boy, not a fucking nature lover. I miss the sound of traffic and the noise of the city. This quiet is hard to take. The sound of that lonely loon calling every day drives me, looney. I feel like grabbing a shotgun and putting that fucker out of his misery," Joe laughed.

"I guess we shouldn't complain," Carmen said. "This is a hell of a lot better than being cooped up in a small jail cell. We're lucky Santino has this cabin, and I'm sure the cops don't even know it exists."

"Yeah, I hate being cooped up. This place is too isolated for my liking. I miss having a woman to care for my needs," Joe laughed.

"That little whore you banged back in Boston wasn't half bad. She certainly had a nice pair of knockers and a tight little ass," Carmen laughed. "I was tempted to go after her twin sister, but I never got around to it."

"Why don't we have Mario fly them up? I'm getting horny as hell. We could have a little party. What do you think?" Joe asked.

"Sounds like a good idea. It would help to pass the time. I'm sick of staring at your ugly face every day." Carmen grinned.

"The feeling's mutual, brother," Joe chuckled. "The only problem is that with no phone service, we'll have to wait till Mario comes back with supplies before we can even ask him about the dames."

"I know what he's going to say—no fucking way! I'm not bringing a couple of whores up here for you two to get your jollies. It's too risky."

"It is too risky. The fewer people who know where we're at, the less chance we have of getting caught," Joe replied.

"Yeah, you're right," Carmen said. "We'll have to sit tight till the heat dies, and Mario can figure a way to get us to a country where there's no extradition treaty with the United States. The problem is that we wouldn't want to go to any of those fucking countries. Any place we might want to go to, like Mexico, has a treaty, and if we were to get caught, we'd get sent back for trial."

"I can imagine the cops are going crazy looking for us. It was dumb of Santino's boys to cap those two police officers," Joe said.

"Yeah, we're probably gonna get charged with two more fucking murders," Carmen said, swallowing his whiskey.

"Shit," Joe said, "we don't even have a TV to watch to see what's happening in the world or to watch a movie or two. It would be nice to know if the cops are still looking for us."

"Oh, they'll still be looking for us, all right. You can count on that."

"This place only has a few old books, most of which I've already read, and a pile of Playboy magazines. If I look at them, it'll just get me horny." Joe laughed.

"Mario brought enough grub for a month, so we don't have to worry about running out of food anytime soon, and we're well stocked with booze," Carmen said as he gulped from a glass half-filled with straight whiskey.

"What I'd like to do is head to Bangor and get our money from that fucking little bitch, Donna Blackmore. If we could find a way out of here, we could hold her two kids hostage while she transfers a million bucks to our offshore account. If we ever get out of the country, we'll need as much dough as possible to live in style," Joe said.

"Maybe we should go and check out the garage and see what's inside."

"Good idea, big brother," Joe agreed. "Let's go take a gander."

When they opened the door, they were surprised to see an almost new black Jeep Wrangler with a red canoe tied to the roof.

"Well, look at that," Carmen beamed. "It looks like we've found our ride out of here. This thing wouldn't be here without a way in and out by land. It's funny Mario never mentioned it, and I thought the only way to get here was by float plane."

"He never mentioned it because he didn't want us getting any ideas about leaving this place," Joe said.

"Yeah, you're right. This vehicle is a real beauty. There must be a map somewhere that shows the way out of here."

Carmen found the manual in the glove box. Tucked inside the manual was a hand-drawn map. He picked it up and began to read.

"Holy shit, someone drew a map with directions over old logging roads. The arrows point the way to Highway 11. The manual says it's a 2014 Jeep Wrangler with four-wheel drive. It's our ticket out of here. Now, all we have to do is find the keys."

"Look," Joe said, "two jerry cans." He lifted each can. "They're both filled with gas."

"That's great," Carmen said. "We should have plenty of fuel to get us to Highway 11, where we can find a gas station and fill this sweetheart up."

"Hey, I found the keys. They were under the floor mat," Joe said, all excited. "Let's see if this baby will start."

He slid behind the steering wheel and turned the key. At first, nothing happened. He pumped the gas pedal twice and tried again. This time, to his amazement, the engine caught, coughed a couple of times and then ran smoothly. "Holy shit, it purrs like a kitten," he said with a big grin. "The fuel gauge shows almost a full tank."

Joe killed the engine and got out.

"Joe, my boy, let's go back to the cabin and have a drink to celebrate our freedom," Carmen said, smiling.

CHAPTER 28

The brothers were up early, excited to get going. The previous night they had studied the hand-drawn map. It looked simple enough. By following the arrows over the old unused logging roads, they would eventually come out on Highway 11. From there, they would head south to I-95 and find a motel near Bangor.

After a hardy breakfast, Joe made two ham and cheese sandwiches, and Carmen filled a cooler with beer and ice, then he put two bottles of Jack Daniels into a canvas grocery bag. They each packed a suitcase with personal effects and clothing, and before leaving, Joe grabbed a telescopic hunting rifle and a pump shotgun with ammunition for each weapon. Mario had picked up their Beretta pistols from their house safe and five thousand dollars in cash and had given his uncles the guns and money during the flight. Joe found a tackle box and two fishing rods, and they packed everything into the jeep. Their newly grown beards disguised their faces, and the canoe mounted on the roof gave the appearance of two fishermen on vacation.

Before leaving, Carmen shut off the generator and locked the cabin door while Joe fired up the Jeep and backed it out of the garage. Carmen slid onto the shotgun seat, clutching the map in his hand. Joe put the Wrangler in gear, and they were on their way.

"If Mario finds out we've left the cabin, he won't be too happy," Carmen said.

"What he doesn't know won't hurt him," Joe laughed. "Besides, he won't be back for a week or so, and we should be back in a few days."

"Let's hope so. If Santino discovers what we're up to, we'll be in deep shit."

"I don't even want to think about it," Joe shuddered. "Let's concentrate on getting the money."

They drove in silence as Carmen read the map.

"Turn right at the next side road," Carmen said.

"Okay, you're the navigator."

Joe turned right at the next side road. As the Jeep bumped along in the badly rutted tracks, the brothers bounced in their seats like a couple of beachballs.

"Are you sure we're on the right road?" Joe asked.

"Yeah, I'm sure. Quit your fucking complaining. You can be the navigator, and I'll do the driving."

"Don't get your shit in a knot. I was only asking. It seems the road is getting worse, and all we'd need is to get stuck out in the middle of fucking nowhere."

"We won't get stuck. That's why these vehicles have four-wheel drive. Besides, I threw a shovel in the back just in case."

"Good thinking."

They drove in silence for fifteen minutes. Suddenly, the road came to a dead end.

"What the fuck," Joe screamed. "Are you sure you read the fucking map right?"

"Yeah, I told you to turn left, and you must have turned right instead."

"Are you fucking kidding me? You must be getting senile. You told me to turn right back there."

"No, I'm sure I told you to turn left."

Frustrated, Joe yelled, "Fuck, fuck, fuck," as he slowly began to turn the Wrangler around.

Neither of them spoke until they were back on the correct road.

"Sorry, little brother," Carmen finally said, "This map's a little blurry and hard to read. I forgot to bring my reading glasses."

"When will you admit that without your glasses, you're as blind as a fucking bat? I'll be glad when we get the fuck out of here and back to civilization."

"Yeah, I can't wait for a hot shower and a few stiff drinks," Carmen grinned.

"I'll drink to that," Joe said, releasing his tension with a hearty laugh.

"Why wait? Sounds like a good idea," Carmen said. He reached into the back seat and pulled a bottle of JD from the bag. He poured a couple of shots into plastic glasses, handed one to Joe, and said, "Salute."

"Salute," Joe said, downing his drink in one gulp.

Two hours later, feeling no pain, and after almost getting stuck a couple of times, they reached Highway 11, switched drivers, and headed south toward I-95.

Near Portage, Maine, Carmen pulled into a mom-and-pop convenience store with gas pumps. "I've got to take a leak," he said. "Why don't you top it up? Don't use a credit card. Pay with cash. We don't want the cops tracing our movements."

"Okay, but I gotta take a leak, too. I'll go when you get back."

Joe went into the store to prepay for the gas and handed the young female clerk fifty dollars. He was about to return to the pumps when he spotted a poster on the wall behind the counter. A wanted poster with his and Carmen's picture offered a reward of $25,000 for information leading to their arrest.

He pulled down his hat, lowered his head, turned abruptly, hurried back to the pumps, and began filling the tank. When Carmen arrived, Joe whispered, "Did you see the poster on the bulletin board in the store?"

"No. What poster?"

"Our wanted poster—they're offering a $25,000 reward for information leading to our arrest."

"Holy shit," Carmen laughed. "We're worth double that amount. Do you think the clerk recognized you?"

"I don't think so. With our beards and caps, we don't look anything like the picture."

"We'd better get the hell out of here before we get spotted," Carmen said, sliding behind the wheel.

When the tank was full, Joe replaced the hose and quickly slid into the passenger seat. "Hey, I still haven't had my piss," he complained.

"You'll have to hold it until we get down the road. I'll stop in a few miles, and you can run into the woods."

"Okay, but make it quick. I've got to go so bad that I might piss my pants if I don't relieve myself soon."

Two and a half hours later, they were pulling into a small run-down motel on the outskirts of Bangor.

An older gray-haired man with a ruddy round face and a long nose sat on a chair behind the front desk reading The Bangor Daily News.

He looked up as Carmen approached.

The man coughed and smiled, showing tobacco-stained teeth. In a raspy smoker's voice, he said, "Howdy, mister, welcome to the Sleepy Hollow Motel. Chester Peabody at your service. How can I help you?"

"I'd like a room with two double beds for a couple of nights," Carmen replied.

"Just for you?"

"No. Not just for me. It's for my brother and me. He's out in the car. What fucking difference does it make if it's for one or two?"

"It costs more for two than for one," the old man said. "It's ten bucks extra per night. If it were just you, it would be forty bucks a night—but for the two of you, it's fifty bucks a night for one hundred bucks for two nights."

"Whatever," Carmen said, irritated with the old geezer's rambling.

He stood up and handed Carmen a registration card and a pen.

"You need to fill in this card, sir. Would you prefer the ground or the second level? Do you want smoking or non-smoking?"

"Let's forget the registration bullshit. I'll give you one hundred and fifty bucks, and you can pocket the extra fifty as a tip. A ground floor room in the back where we can park in front of the door would be good. Give us a smoking room."

Putting a hand over his eyes, he said, "I'll pretend you're not even here." He laughed and gave a yellow-toothed grin.

"Fucking asshole," Carmen mumbled under his breath. He handed the man a hundred and fifty bucks. In return, he received the key to room 115.

After throwing their belongings into the reasonably clean but dingy room, Carmen headed outside to the ice machine. Joe retrieved the half-empty bottle of Jack and placed it on a small, wooden table. When Carmen returned, Joe turned over the two glasses supplied by the motel, threw in some ice, poured two double shots, handed Carmen his glass, and said, "Here's to happy hunting—salute."

"Salute," Carmen said. They touched glasses and downed their drinks.

After a few more shots, they showered and changed into fresh clothes.

"Now that I feel human again, I'm hungry as hell. I could eat the ass out of a monkey," Joe said, laughing. "Let's head to the McDonald's we passed down the road."

"You mean you can eat the ass out of a skunk," Carmen grinned.

"Who gives a shit if it's a monkey or a skunk? I'm just fucking starving."

"Sounds good. I could use a little grub myself—my stomach's growling like a junkyard dog. We'd better use the drive-through. If we go inside, we might get recognized," Carmen cautioned.

"Yeah, you're right. There's no telling where the cops planted those fucking wanted posters. We'd better not take any unnecessary chances. We can bring the food back here and wash it down with a few beers."

"Good idea," Carmen agreed.

A half-hour later, they were back at the motel with four cheeseburgers and two boxes of fries. They attacked the food like starving wolves devouring a freshly killed deer. After a few beers,

Carmen said, "Let's drive to the Blackmore house and reconnoiter the joint."

"Good idea, big brother," Joe said. "Sounds like you're getting high and mighty on me using the fancy word reconnoiter. Why don't you just say, let's take a look?" They laughed hardily. Three sheets to the wind, they put on their jackets and headed out the door.

After Carmen had left, the desk clerk continued to read his newspaper. He spotted an article on an inside page that caught his attention. SUSPECTS ESCAPE, TWO COPS KILLED. The article described the brutal killing of two Boston police officers. It said their SUV was attacked as it was leaving Boston for Bangor. Joseph Alberto Catalini and Carmen Antonio Catalini, murder suspects in the killing of local All-Star Realty, Inc. owner Wayne Daniel Blackmore, were whisked away in a stolen white van. A reward of $25,000 was being offered for information leading to the arrest of the two suspects. A picture of the brothers stared back at him. Readers were asked to call a toll-free number and to report any sightings to the police. The last line cautioned that the suspects were considered armed and dangerous—and were not to be approached directly.

"Holy crap," he said aloud. One of the men looked familiar. "No wonder he paid cash and didn't want to fill in the registration card."

Excited, he dropped the newspaper on the counter and opened the top right-hand drawer of his desk. He removed the wanted poster and studied it carefully. The eyes in the picture were the same mean-looking, beady eyes of the man who had paid cash for room 115. The other man, his brother, looked similar. Both men had greasy dark hair flecked with gray. They looked like the type of characters you wouldn't want to cross. They looked like the stereotypical gangsters you saw on TV and in the movies.

Forgetting his arthritis, the clerk jumped up and scampered out the door. He cautiously crept around the building clutching the wanted poster in his hand. Staying low, he hid behind a car a few parking spaces from room 115. Parked in front of the door, he saw a black Jeep Wrangler with a red wooden canoe mounted on the roof. To his surprise, a few minutes later, the door opened, and the two men appeared. He recognized the man who had paid for the room. It was hard to tell if they were the men in the newspaper picture. Their camouflage hunting caps and beards placed a sliver of doubt in his mind. However, when he glanced at the wanted poster, any doubt he had disappeared. They were definitely the fugitives wanted by the police!

As the two men drove away, he yanked out a small pad and pen from his shirt pocket and quickly jotted down the Massachusetts plate number, then he rushed back to the office. With a wide grin, he grabbed the newspaper and, looking at the article, began dialing the toll-free number. In his mind, he was already spending the reward money.

The sun was beginning to sink when the Catalini brothers reached the Blackmore residence. Joe pulled the Jeep onto the shoulder just before the long, circular driveway. Getting out, they quietly closed the doors. Crouching low, they slowly made their way to one of the sentry-like stone pillars on either side of the driveway entrance.

Peering around the pillar, Joe said, "Looks like they're expecting us. There's a police cruiser sitting in the driveway in front of the house, and it looks like two cops are keeping guard."

The front door opened, Donna Blackmore came out carrying a tray, and she handed the driver two cups. She spoke briefly to the officers, then turned and returned to the house.

"It looks like that bitch brought the cops coffee, but she forgot the doughnuts. She must be trying to keep them awake for the night shift," Joe said, chuckling.

"Shit," whispered Carmen. "We can't just walk up to the house and surprise her. We'll have to figure out how to take care of the cops."

CHAPTER 29

T he Barkowsky family and Buck had just finished dinner when Jim's cell phone vibrated.

"Detective Barkowsky," he said without checking the screen.

"Hi, Jim, it's Chief Durham. I just received a call from the Maine State Police informing me that the Catalini brothers may be in Bangor. The desk clerk at the Sleepy Hollow Motel thinks they could be staying in room 115. He said they left driving a black Jeep Wrangler with Massachusetts plates a short time ago. The Jeep has a red wooden canoe on the roof. They didn't appear to be in a hurry. My guess is they'll be going back to the motel. The clerk wrote down the plate number; the vehicle is registered to Mario Morano from Boston. He's one of Santino Morano's boys. The Maine State Police are sending a SWAT team to the motel shortly. Do you and Buck want to join them?"

"Yes, sir, we do."

After hanging up, Jim updated Buck and informed Shawna where they were going.

As they headed for the door, Shawna yelled, "Be careful, you two. Don't take any unnecessary chances!"

"Don't worry, we'll be fine," Jim shouted.

Buck ran to his truck, grabbed his Glock and badge from the glove box, and hurried to Jim's idling car. Jim turned on the siren and hit the gas. Tires screamed, and rubber smoked as the car fishtailed down the road headed for I-95.

"From what the chief said, the Catalini brothers left the motel about an hour ago. Where do you think they were heading?" Jim asked.

"Maybe they were going to grab a bite to eat," Buck said. He paused for a few seconds, thinking. Then it came to him! "Shit, I bet they went to Donna Blackmore's house."

"From what the chief said, they weren't spooked. I don't think they were leaving the motel for good."

"Since the SWAT team will be at the motel, it might be wise for us to swing past the Blackmore residence just to ensure things are okay," Buck suggested.

"Good idea. The Bangor PD is watching the house, but it wouldn't hurt to double-check to see if things are all right."

Jim cut the siren as they exited I-95. Ten minutes later, they parked behind a black Jeep Wrangler with a red canoe on the roof.

"Holy shit! Good call, Buck. It looks like you were right. The brothers are here."

They got out of the car and crept up to the driveway entrance. In the darkness, they could make out the shape of a police cruiser stationed in front of the main entrance. It was quiet, and everything looked completely normal.

"I don't see any sign of life," Jim said.

"We're too far away," Buck whispered. "We've got to get closer. Follow me."

Buck's Marine training kicked in. He got down on his belly on the grass to the right of the driveway and began to slither like a snake. Jim did the same, and five minutes later; they were behind the police car. Keeping low, Buck crept to the driver's door and peeked through the window. The car was empty.

Jim was right behind him. He peered into the car and said, "What the hell happened to the two officers?"

"The Catalini brothers—that's what happened to them," Buck said in a low whisper.

"Shit, the brothers must've surprised them and used the officers to get inside the house. Well, at least they didn't kill them. At least, I hope not."

"You're probably right. I bet the brothers forced one of the officers to ring the bell. When Donna saw the officer, she opened the door, and they barged in on her," Buck surmised.

"That makes sense," Jim agreed. "They're probably going to get her to transfer money to their offshore account in the morning."

"Let's sneak around to the family room window. I'm sure that's where they'll be," Buck said.

"Okay. Lead the way."

When they reached the family room window, Buck peered in and saw what he expected. The two police officers were each duct-taped to kitchen chairs in the middle of the room. Donna Blackmore and her boys, Billy and Bobby, sat on the couch with tears streaming down their faces. Their wrists and ankles were duct-taped like the two police officers. The Catalini brothers stood in front of the Blackmore family.

Jim peeked in the window just as Carmen, waving his pistol, yelled, "You bitch, you thought you could outsmart us. Calling in the cops was a dumb move." He walked over to Donna and slapped her face with his hand. Her head jerked sideways from the vicious blow, and blood dripped from her nose. Still crying, Bobby and Billy's eyes widened in fear.

"Tomorrow morning, as soon as the bank opens, you'll transfer a million dollars into our offshore account, or else you're all going to die," Joe screamed.

"In the meantime," Carmen said, "let's make ourselves comfy. It's gonna be a long night."

"What's our plan?" Jim asked.

"I'm working on it. Do you think the police officers check in with dispatch periodically?"

"Yeah, that should be normal procedure. That way, the station knows everything's okay."

"Do you think the brothers will know that?"

"I don't know. I guess we'll soon find out. Should we call and have the SWAT team diverted over here?" Jim asked.

"Not yet. If SWAT comes charging in, someone could die, and I don't want it to be Donna and her boys."

Five minutes later, Joe looked at his watch and said, "It's time to report in." He removed the tape from the female officer and marched her out of the room at gunpoint.

"Holy shit," Jim said, "that answers your question. He's bringing the officer out to the cruiser to check in."

Quickly, they returned to the front of the house, and, just in time, they hid behind high shrubs near the entrance. The door opened, and they watched as the officer and Joe headed to the police cruiser. The female officer slid behind the wheel and radioed Bangor PD dispatch.

"Dispatch," a husky male voice said.

"This is Officer Shannon Murdoch, reporting in from the stakeout at the Blackmore residence. All is quiet—nothing to report. Over and out."

"Copy that. Over and out," the dispatcher said.

Officer Murdoch slid out of the car under the watchful eye of Joe Catalini. With his pistol pressed into her back, he nudged her toward the front door. Buck snuck up behind him without making a sound and placed his Glock on the back of his head.

"Hand over your gun if you want to live," Buck whispered into his ear.

"Okay, okay, don't shoot." He lowered the pistol to his side, and Jim grabbed the gun out of his hand.

Relieved, Officer Murdoch said, "I don't know who you guys are, but I'm glad you're here."

"I'm Detective Jim Barkowsky of the Orono PD, and this is my friend and acting partner Detective Buck Woods from the NYPD."

"I'm Officer Shannon Murdoch. Pleased to meet you both."

Jim turned to Buck and asked, "What's the plan?"

"The plan is not to get anyone killed. Somehow we've got to get Carmen to the front door."

"How are we going to do that?" Jim asked.

"Joe, if you value your life, I want you to do this," Buck said. He proceeded to outline his plan.

When they were ready, Joe opened the door. Buck and Jim stood out of view on either side of him with their guns ready.

"Carmen," Joe shouted, "I need your help."

"What's goin' on?" Carmen yelled back.

"It's that stupid female officer. She tried to grab my gun, and I had to whack her on the head. I need you to help carry her back inside."

"Shit," Carmen grumbled, "can't you fucking do anything right?"

Carmen put his pistol into a coat pocket and hurried down the hallway. Joe stepped aside so Carmen could see the motionless body of the female police officer lying on the driveway. As Carmen stepped outside, he said, "She's not moving. You didn't kill her, did you?"

"No, she's just unconscious," Joe replied.

"Put your hands above your head," Buck barked.

Surprised, Carmen stopped dead in his tracks. "What the fuck," he bellowed.

Very much alive, Officer Murdoch got up off the driveway.

"The two of you are under arrest for loan sharking, extortion, and the murder of Wayne Daniel Blackmore," Jim said. He read them their Miranda rights while Buck disarmed Carmen and snapped handcuffs on both brothers.

Joe hollered, "We're innocent. Blackmore was already dead when we got there."

"Yeah, that's what they all say," Jim said.

"We want our lawyer," Carmen yelled.

"In due time," Buck said. "You'll get your phone call from jail."

After placing the brothers in the back of the cruiser, Buck said, "Here, Officer Murdoch, take my gun. Keep an eye on these scumbags while Detective Barkowsky and I go inside and free your partner and the Blackmore family."

"My pleasure, Detective," she replied.

Buck removed the duct tape from the police officer.

"Thanks," he said. "I'm Officer Tim Owen. Where's my partner?"

"She's outside guarding the scumbags," Buck said. "They're cuffed and in the back of your cruiser."

Buck introduced himself and Jim, and they shook Officer Owen's hand.

Jim removed the duct tape from Donna, while Buck did the same for Billy and Bobby.

"Thank God you got here in time, Detectives, Donna said." Her swollen eyes filled with tears, and blood still dripped from her nose.

Jim fished out a clean handkerchief and handed it to Donna. "You and the boys are safe now," he said.

Relief written on her face, dabbing at her bloody nose, Donna sobbed, "Once they got the money transferred in the morning, I'm sure they weren't going to leave any witnesses."

"They won't bother you again. They'll be going away for a long time and will probably die in prison," Buck said.

Officer Owen picked up their pistols off the coffee table and said, "I guess I'd better help Officer Murdoch get those two greaseballs to jail where they belong."

"To be safe, we'll follow you in my car," Jim said.

Buck gave Jim the two .38 caliber Beretta handguns from the Catalini brothers.

"I'll have these guns sent to the crime lab in the morning. I'm sure one of them will turn out to be the weapon that killed Wayne Blackmore," Jim said.

"If one of them is the murder weapon," Buck said, "that should put the final nail in their coffins."

After the Catalini brothers were booked into the Penobscot County Jail, Buck and Jim headed home, exhausted and relieved.

CHAPTER 30

The following morning at nine, Jim, Buck, and Captain Tony Timpano met in Chief Durham's office. After Jim told the story about the capture of the Catalini brothers, the chief said, "Good work, Detectives. While the Maine State Police SWAT team spun their wheels at the motel, you two arrested the suspects at the Blackmore residence."

"It was Buck's idea to go there first," Jim said. "It turned out to be the right decision."

"Jim's being modest, Chief," Buck said. "It was a team effort, and he's one hell of a detective."

Why didn't you call the SWAT team when you discovered the Catalini brothers were at Donna Blackmore's house?" Captain Timpano asked.

"We decided to see if we could devise a plan without causing too much confusion. Buck had an idea, and it worked. Things could have gone south if the SWAT team had come rushing in, and we didn't want to take that chance unless we had to. Luckily, it worked out, and no one got hurt," Jim said.

"Again, gentlemen, I commend you for your excellent work. For your information, I contacted Chief O'Brien and gave him the name of Mario Morano, the owner of the vehicle the suspects were driving. The Boston PD is picking Morano up and charging him with aiding and abetting in the escape of the suspects. Mario Morano may not have been one of the shooters, but the Boston PD suspects he or his father were involved in planning the attack. I know Chief O'Brien won't rest until those responsible for the ambush and brutal murder of his two officers are collared and brought to justice," Chief Durham said.

"That's good to hear," Captain Timpano said. "I'd also like to thank both of you for your excellent work."

"Thanks, Captain," Jim and Buck said in unison.

"I'm having an officer drive the two pistols of the suspects to the crime lab this morning. We should have the results in a day or two."

"I'm betting that one of those two guns killed Wayne Blackmore," Jim said.

"I hope you're right." Glancing at his watch, the chief said, "Jim, you and Buck had better get moving if you want to get to Bangor on time for Brenda's and Rusty's arraignments."

"You're right, Chief," Jim said. "Let's go, Buck."

Buck and Jim arrived at the courthouse ten minutes before Brenda's scheduled arraignment time of ten-thirty and sat in the back row.

Her head down, Brenda, handcuffed, wearing an orange prison uniform, looked pale and exhausted. She sat next to her lawyer, Kaleb Swartz, who wore a rumpled blue suit, a wrinkled white shirt, and a red tie. His black shoes were scuffed and unpolished.

Assistant DA Paul Prentice sat across the aisle at a table to Kaleb's right with a notepad in front of him. In contrast to Kaleb, Prentice was immaculately dressed. He wore a tailored dark-gray suit that looked recently pressed, a freshly starched white shirt, a light-gray tie, and his black loafers gleamed.

At precisely ten thirty, Judge Calvin Roberts entered the courtroom.

"All rise. The court is now in session. The honorable judge Calvin G. Roberts presiding," the bailiff said.

Everyone stood.

"Please be seated," the judge said, squeezing into his chair.

Everyone sat down.

To say Judge Roberts was a huge man would be a vast understatement. Obese would be more suitable. He had to weigh close to 300 pounds. His bald head glistened from the reflection of the overhead fluorescent lighting. His round, red face with a double chin looked like he could suffer a stroke or heart attack any minute. His small beady, laser-like brown eyes gave the impression that he could see through you.

He coughed into his hand, took a sip of water, cleared his throat, and said, "Will the defendant please rise." Brenda and Kaleb stood. Reviewing his notes, he continued. "In the State of Maine versus Brenda Jane Sykes on the charge of voluntary manslaughter in the death of Doreen Patricia Warren, how does the defendant plead?"

"Guilty, Your Honor," Brenda and Kaleb said in unison.

"Are there any questions or statements the defense wants to make now?"

"No, Your Honor," Kaleb said.

"Are there any questions or statements the prosecution wants to make now?"

"No, Your Honor," Paul Prentice stated.

"Since you have pled guilty to the charge of voluntary manslaughter, a bail hearing will not be required. Brenda Jane Sykes, you will be remanded into custody until two weeks from today at two o'clock for sentencing. Two weeks will give me time to review all the facts in this case as presented by the prosecution and the defense. Until that time, this proceeding is adjourned." The judge tapped his gavel, and everyone stood. He pushed himself out of his chair, turned, and Judge Roberts waddled back to his chamber like an overfed duck.

The large clock on the wall in the front of the courtroom showed ten forty-five.

Jim turned to Buck and whispered, "That was fast."

Buck nodded and whispered back, "You got that right. Judge Roberts doesn't waste time."

The bailiff ushered Brenda out of the courtroom and turned her over to a state trooper who would deliver her back to the Penobscot County Jail.

At eleven-twenty, Rusty shuffled into the courtroom assisted by the bailiff. In a prison uniform, handcuffed and wearing leg irons, he took Brenda's previous seat.

Rusty glanced back and gave Jim and Buck an icy glare. Continuing to stare at Buck, he mouthed the word "asshole" and then turned and spoke to Kaleb Swartz. Kaleb nodded and scribbled on his notepad.

At precisely eleven thirty, Judge Roberts reappeared. Once more, the bailiff went through his routine, announcing the judge as he entered the courtroom. After he sat down, the judge asked everyone to be seated.

"Would the defendant please rise?" When Rusty and Kaleb were on their feet, he continued. "In the State of Maine versus Russell Donald Sykes on the charge of intimidating a witness in the death of Doreen Patricia Warren, how does the defendant plead?"

"Guilty, Your Honor," they said.

"Sentencing will take place two weeks from today at three o'clock. The defendant will be held in custody pending a bail hearing scheduled for two o'clock today. Are there any questions or statements from the defense or the prosecution?"

"No, Your Honor," Kaleb Swartz said.

"No, Your Honor," Paul Prentice said.

Judge Roberts tapped his gavel and said, "This proceeding is adjourned."

Jim and Buck stayed in Bangor for lunch, then drove back to the courthouse for Rusty's bail hearing.

At two o'clock, they went through the same ritual. This time the lawyers argued their points for and against bail amounts. Paul Prentice argued for fifty thousand dollars, and Kaleb Swartz asked for half that amount. Ultimately, Judge Roberts decided to grant bail for thirty thousand dollars. Later that same afternoon, with the help of Kaleb Swartz, Rusty managed to post a property bond using his and Brenda's house as collateral. He was released on a promise to appear for sentencing in two weeks.

The following day, Buck and Jim drove back to Bangor for the arraignment of Carmen and Joe Catalini scheduled for two o'clock. They arrived fifteen minutes early and found seats a few rows behind where the brothers sat with Carl Bono, their high-priced Boston Mafia lawyer.

Bono represented the Morano crime family in all criminal matters. In his mid-thirties, he had graduated from Yale law school, second in his class. After graduation, he joined the prestigious Boston law firm of Albani, Carpino & Ferrelli, and within five years, he worked his way into a full partnership. The law firm's name was recently changed to Albani, Carpino, Ferrelli & Bono.

Single, Bono was a handsome man with an athletic build and stood just under six feet. He had short, neatly combed black hair and sparkling brown eyes, and he radiated a cocky self-confidence. Bono always dressed immaculately in tailored blue or gray suits. He was intelligent and a tiger in court. According to rumors in Boston social circles, he was also a tiger in bed. The word on the street— don't cross him!

Bono sat in the middle, with Joe on his left and Carmen on his right. Carmen turned his head and spotted the two arresting detectives, and he nudged Joe, whispered into his ear, and then they both turned and scowled at Buck and Jim.

Prentice once more represented the district attorney's office for the prosecution.

A crowd of newspaper and TV reporters from Bangor and Boston, plus a few towns and cities throughout the state, had filled the courtroom to cover the sensational story.

At two o'clock sharp, Judge Roberts appeared.

The bailiff said, "All rise. The court is now in session, Judge Calvin G. Roberts presiding."

Please be seated," Judge Roberts said as he struggled to fit his oversized body into his chair.

"We are here today for the arraignment of Carmen Antonio Catalini and Joseph Alberto Catalini. Will the defendants please rise?"

When he asked how the defendants pled to the charge of first-degree murder in the death of Wayne Daniel Blackmore, Carl Bono and the Catalini brothers said, "Not guilty, Your Honor."

"Duly noted," the judge said. "In the State of Maine versus Carmen Antonio Catalini and Joseph Alberto Catalini on the charges of loan sharking and extortion in dealings with Wayne Daniel Blackmore and Donna Joan Blackmore, how do the defendants plead?"

Again, they said, "Not guilty, Your Honor."

"Duly noted. Are there any questions or statements the defense wants to make now?"

"No, Your Honor," Carlo Bono said.

"Are there any questions or statements the prosecution wants to make now?"

"No, Your Honor," Paul Prentice said.

"The defendants are to be held in custody until two o'clock tomorrow for a bail hearing in this same courtroom." Judge Roberts pounded his gavel. "This arraignment is now adjourned."

Everyone stood, and he departed.

"Well," Buck said, "it looks like they're going to fight the charges in court."

"I didn't expect anything less," Jim said. "I think we should be here for the bail hearing."

"If they make bail, we'd better be prepared to protect Donna and her family. The brothers may be crazy enough to go after her and her boys again," Buck said.

"You're right. We'd better be prepared just in case."

Buck and Jim were back at the courthouse in Bangor the following afternoon.

Joe and Carmen sat with Carlo Bono, anxiously awaiting the appearance of Judge Roberts.

Punctual as usual, at two, he made his appearance. The bailiff went through his announcement routine, and after Judge Roberts squeezed into his chair, he said, "Please be seated. This bail hearing is now in session." He read the charges and said, "I have carefully reviewed and weighed all of the facts in this case, and since each defendant has a lengthy criminal record, I have concluded that if granted bail, the defendants are a risk to flee. Therefore, I am unable to grant bail for these reasons. The defendants will remain in custody until their trial's conclusion, pending the jury's decision. A trial date will be determined after consultation with the prosecution and the defense. This hearing is now adjourned."

He thumped his gavel loudly, and everyone stood.

Suddenly, Joe and Carmen Catalini jumped up and started yelling.

"Judge, your ruling is unfair," Joe yelled.

"We should be granted bail," Carmen screamed.

"Order in my courtroom," Judge Roberts shouted at the top of his lungs, fiercely pounding his gavel. "Order, or you'll be in contempt."

Carlo Bono ran toward the judge's bench and bellowed, "Your Honor, your decision is unfair. My clients are upstanding citizens and are at no risk to flee, and they should be granted bail pending trial."

Everyone started talking, and the courtroom turned into complete chaos. The media were having a field day, snapping pictures and recording videos.

Once more, Judge Roberts shouted, "Order! Order in my courtroom." He continued pounding his gavel until the head flew off straight at Carlo Bono.

Bono managed to duck just in time. He shouted, "Your Honor, Your Honor, your ruling is unfair."

Judge Roberts glared at him and bellowed, "Another word from you, Attorney Bono, and I'll hold you in contempt." He pointed the gavel handle at Bono and said, "Not one more word, Mr. Bono! Not one more word!"

Bono's mouth froze. It was wide open, but nothing came out.

The bailiff and two state troopers quickly hustled the Catalini brothers out of the courtroom.

As things began to settle down, without another word, Judge Roberts pushed himself out of his chair and shuffled off as fast as he could go, still clutching the gavel handle.

For a brief moment, Buck and Jim stared at one another in silence. Then Jim said, "What the hell was that all about?"

"It was like a three-ring circus," Buck chuckled.

"Thank God they didn't get bail. At least, we'll know where they'll be," Jim said.

"Yeah, the Blackmore family won't have to look over their shoulder worrying about those slimeballs," Buck said.

Most reporters were chasing Carlo Bono, asking for his comments. Ignoring their questions, Bono rushed out the door toward his waiting limousine. Before getting into the vehicle, he yelled, "An injustice has been served here today. I have no further comment. Thank you, and good day!" He slid into the back seat, slammed the door, and the limousine sped away.

After Bono made his escape, Jim and Buck became the center of attention. Hungry reporters surrounded them, and questions began to fly.

"Detective Barkowsky," Sharon Cox of TV News 5 asked, shoving a microphone in front of Jim's face, "do you have any comments about the Catalini brothers not being granted bail?"

"Yes, Ms. Cox, I do have a few comments. I agree wholeheartedly with the decision of Judge Roberts. In my opinion, keeping those criminals off the streets until the verdict of their trial is the safest thing to do. Now, if you'll excuse me."

Jim and Buck elbowed through the crowd, ignoring several other questions.

The following morning, Jim's phone rang. It was the crime lab.

"Good morning, Detective Barkowsky," Jim said.

"Hi, Jim. Sorry for not getting back to you sooner," Dr. Corey Chambers said. "We've been trying to identify the prints on the bag and packages of heroin. We searched all the databases and came up empty. As we were about to give up, Doug Graham suggested we check them against the prints he took from Wayne Blackmore, and we got a hit. In a way, it makes sense since he was at the cabin, and it looks like he was the one who buried the drugs under the living room floor. The bag has been turned over to the Maine Drug Enforcement Agency. Testing confirmed that the drugs are heroin."

"Interesting," Jim said. "It's hard to believe Wayne Blackmore was a drug dealer."

"We identified the prints on the dustpan and broom as belonging to Mr. Joseph Catalini. As for the two .38 caliber Beretta handguns obtained from your suspects, I'm sorry, neither gun matched the slug removed from the victim. I'll send you the report ASAP. That's it for now, Jim. Take care."

"Thanks, Dr. Chambers."

They said goodbye and hung up.

Jim began to mull everything over in his mind. *I can't believe the slug in Wayne Blackmore didn't match either of the Catalini pistols. What the fuck is going on? Did they kill him with another gun that they tossed? After all, they did say they killed Wayne Blackmore on the recording. Maybe they were bluffing, trying to scare Donna Blackmore to get her money. If they didn't kill Wayne Blackmore, then who did? No, they must have killed him with another gun. Why would they say they killed him if they didn't?*

The prints of Joe Catalini on the broom handle and dustpan proved they were at the cabin. He must have swept the floor after they killed Wayne Blackmore. Was Blackmore going to use the proceeds from the sale of the heroin to repay his gambling debt? If he was, he never got the chance.

If Blackmore had told them about the heroin, maybe they still would have killed him and taken the drugs. It was a no-win situation for Wayne Blackmore. *Shit! Things are getting extremely complicated! This case is starting to drive me crazy. I could use a stiff drink!*

CHAPTER 31

Rusty sat in his car smoking pot, watching people come and go from the Home Depot. The muscle spasms in his lower back felt like a sharp needle was jabbing him. The weed did little to alleviate the pain or calm his agitated mind. Periodically he would glance at Brenda's Lady Smith & Wesson lying on the passenger seat.

While he waited, Rusty's thoughts drifted back to his teenage days. *How I wish I'd had a gun back then. I could've used it the night I came home after celebrating my fifteenth birthday with my friends.*

As he walked through the door, the terrified voice of his mother pleaded, "Please, please stop!"

Kneeling on the living room floor, Rusty's mother crossed her arms, trying to shield her face. His father stood over her with a belt in his right hand. Without a word, he viciously struck her three times on the head.

Before he could strike her again, Rusty raced into the room and tackled his father hard from behind, knocking him to the floor. Enraged, the big man staggered to his feet, turned, and began to use the belt on Rusty.

He snarled, "Don't you interfere, boy. Your mother had it comin'."

After whipping Rusty a few more times, his dad stopped, dropped the belt, and staggered into the bedroom. He fell onto the bed, passing out instantly.

Rusty ran to his mother, and they clung to one another with tears flowing down their cheeks.

Not wanting anyone to see his welts and bruises, Rusty played hooky from school for a few days. His mother signed a note saying he had been sick with a bad cold.

Rusty remembered how badly he had wanted to run away from home but couldn't bring himself to leave his mother with that monster.

Rusty glanced at the clock on the dashboard; it was almost ten— closing time!

A few minutes later, employees gradually began to emerge from the building. He spotted Terry Wells leaving the main entrance at twelve minutes past ten. Rusty picked up the .38 and slipped it into the pocket of his windbreaker. He slid out of the car and followed Terry. Rusty silently came up behind him as Terry was about to unlock the car door and poked the gun into his back.

"Hi, Terry, long time no see," Rusty cackled with a sadistic laugh. "Couldn't keep your big mouth shut, could you."

Terry froze—he could barely speak. He stammered, "Wha.... what do you want, Rus-Rus-ty?"

Once more, Rusty laughed and said, "What I want is to teach you a lesson for not takin' me seriously that night at the river. Remember when I said you'd be dead meat if you opened your big mouth about what you saw that night? You should've listened, Terry."

"I'm sorry, Rusty. I should've listened. I don't know what I was thinking."

"It's too late for sorry, Terry. Put your hands behind your back, or I'll put a bullet through your thick skull right now."

Terry complied, and when his hands were behind his back, Rusty snapped on a pair of handcuffs.

Rusty thought. Sometimes being a cop has its advantages.

"Now turn around and walk," Rusty said.

When they got to his car, Rusty looked around, and no one was watching. He opened the trunk and demanded, "Get in, Terry. If you utter one peep, I'll stop the fuckin' car and shoot you on the spot," he said, slamming the trunk lid.

For the first thirty minutes, the car rode smoothly. Suddenly, it slowed and made a left turn. For several seconds, Terry bounced around like a beach ball. The definitive pinging of stones and gravel crunching indicated they were on a dirt road. Seconds later, the car came to a complete stop.

Rusty slid out of the seat and began to sing the Rollins Band song, "Liar." He sang off-key and was doing a good job butchering the lyrics.

CHAPTER 32

Jim and Buck sat relaxing in the family room, each sipping a beer. Kristina, Nicolas, and Shawna had retired for the night after a long day.

Jim had just finished telling Buck that the fingerprints on the bag of heroin belonged to Wayne Blackmore and that the prints on the broom and dustpan matched Joe Catalini when the phone rang.

Jim glanced at his watch. It was a few minutes after eleven. "I wonder who's calling at this hour?" The name on the screen was Terry Wells.

Jim said, "B.J., it must be for you. It's Terry Wells."

Without answering, he handed the phone to Buck.

Buck looked puzzled. Why would Terry be calling him? What could he want at this time of night?

"Hey, Terry, what's up?"

"Hi, Buckley, old buddy," Rusty said with a psychotic laugh.

"Sykes, what the hell do you want?" Buck said, clearly annoyed.

"Does your truck ride better with four new tires?" Rusty said, laughing.

"You crazy fuck, Sykes. I knew it was you. When I get my hands on you, I'll wring your fucking neck."

"Gee, Buckley, you don't sound happy to hear from me. Suddenly, Rusty became agitated. He demanded. "Why the fuck were you and Barkowsky in court today. Are you playin' detective out of your jurisdiction? Why don't you fuck off back to New York?" He became mellow again. "You did a nice job fixin' up your cabin. I think it's really nice."

"What the hell are you doing in my cabin, you idiot?"

"Watch your temper. You're liable to have a heart attack. Do you want to play hero and come and save your little friend, Terry Wells?"

"What's going on, Rusty? What are you talking about?"

"I brought Terry on a little tour so he could see all the stuff you bought from him. He appears quite impressed, and I think he wants to tell you himself."

As Jim listened to the conversation, he understood what was happening.

There was a brief pause, and then Buck heard, "Bu-Bu-Buck, it's Ter-Ter-ry. I'm at your ca-ca-bin with Rus-Rus-ty."

Before he could say another word, Rusty returned and said, "Ain't it like old times, Buckley, me, pickin' on poor little Terry, and you wantin' to save him." Suddenly, Rusty's tone changed, and his voice turned venomous. "You got until midnight to get your ass out here, or you'll be cleanin' another corpse off your nice new floor. You'd better come alone and don't be late, or Terry will be history. If I see any cops or Jim Barkowsky, Terry's dead meat—understand?"

Before Buck could reply, Rusty had hung up.

Shocked and angry, Buck's face turned red with rage. Staring at Jim, he said, "That fucking maniac has kidnapped Terry Wells and is holding him at my cabin. He's giving me until midnight and said he'll kill Terry if I don't arrive on time."

"Holy shit, I'll go with you, partner."

"He said no cops, especially you. I can't take that chance. He's gone off the deep end, and I don't think he's bluffing."

"I can set you up with a wireless communication device. It's a new piece of equipment the chief wants me to test. It's a two-way radio recorder that attaches to your wrist and uses a tiny earbud. I'll stay out of sight and be there to back you up. That way, we can talk without Rusty knowing, and I can hear everything that's going on between you and him. In the dark, he won't be able to detect it."

"I don't know. Are you sure it'll work without Rusty finding out?"

"I guarantee it'll work. Rusty won't have a clue."

Okay, but make sure he can't see you. There's no way I want to jeopardize Terry's life."

After attaching the recorders to their wrists and putting in the earbuds, a quick test proved that everything worked perfectly.

Buck checked his watch, eleven fourteen. "It's about six miles to the cabin. We don't have much time," he said, an anxious look on his face.

"You're right! We'd better get our asses in gear," Jim agreed.

They made a mad dash to Buck's truck and flew out of the driveway onto Perk O'Rock Landing Road, spraying gravel from the spinning tires. Reaching Forest Avenue, barely stopping, Buck made a quick right turn and floored the accelerator. A few minutes later, Forest Avenue turned into Orono Road. The truck fishtailed around a sharp right-hand turn when they reached Pushaw Road. Up ahead, a male deer with large antlers, mesmerized, stood in the middle of the road, staring directly into the headlights. Instinctively, Buck slammed on the brakes and spun the wheel to avoid hitting the animal. He narrowly missed the deer, and it loped off into the woods. The truck did a three-sixty, rocked violently, and came close to flipping over. A loud bang echoed in their ears as the rear tires slid sideways, hitting the gravel shoulder. A few seconds later, the truck came to a complete stop.

They had been holding their breath. Exhaling loudly, both of them began to shake.

"What the fuck was that," Jim yelled. "It sounded like a gunshot."

"I think we just blew a tire," Buck said, his knuckles white on the steering wheel.

"That was close! I thought for sure we were going to flip. It scared the living shit out of me," Jim said, sweat dripping from his forehead.

"Scared the shit out of me, too," Buck said, "We'd better survey the damage. There's a flashlight in the glove compartment. Grab it, and let's take a look."

The right rear tire was flatter than a pancake. Nothing else appeared to be damaged.

Glancing at his watch, Buck said, "Shit, we've got less than thirty minutes to get there. If we're one minute late, I'm sure that maniac will kill Terry."

"Then we don't have a second to waste. Do you have a spare tire?"

"Yeah, there's a full-size spare in the back," Buck said.

The clock was ticking! Working as fast as they could, removing the blown tire and putting on the spare still took fifteen minutes.

Rechecking his watch, Buck said, "We've got less than ten minutes. Let's pray we make it on time!"

They jumped back into the truck and took off as fast as the road would allow. Buck made the sharp turn onto Lakeside Landing Road on two wheels. They were almost there!

After letting Jim out at the entrance, Buck started down the winding gravel laneway. He pulled in behind Rusty's car and cut the engine. It was precisely 11:58 p.m., and he prayed he wasn't too late!

Buck had his Glock tucked into his waist behind his back. He paused for a few seconds to check in with Jim, and they could hear each other loud and clear.

As he stepped down from the truck, everything looked quiet. A few seconds later, Rusty opened the door, standing behind Terry, holding a gun to his head.

Rusty glanced at his watch, and sounding disappointed; he said, "You made it just in time, Buckley. Poor little Terry has been shittin' bricks waitin' for you. It's nice of you to join the party, asshole. You'd better have come alone, or Terry will be history."

"Yeah, I'm alone. What are you trying to prove, Sykes? Have you gone completely mad?"

"You think I'm crazy, do you?"

"I don't think you're crazy. I know you're crazy, Sykes. Let Terry go, and I'll take his place."

"And why should I do that? Terry betrayed me when he opened his big yap about what happened to your sweet little girlfriend, Doreen Warren."

"This beef is between you and me. Let Terry go. I'll take his place. Don't do anything you're going to regret."

Terry had been trembling all this time. He looked like he was about to shit his pants or faint—maybe both.

Rusty pondered for a minute. "Okay, Buckley, that sounds fair.

Get your ass up here and throw your gun away. I know it's on you. It's probably stashed behind your back."

Good guess! He hoped that Jim had heard everything. Buck's long hair covered the earbud, and his long-sleeve shirt hid the wristband. He reached behind, pulled out his Glock, and tossed it on the ground.

Rusty cautiously pulled Terry back, away from the door. He had his left arm around his chest, and in his right hand, he held a pistol to Terry's head.

As Buck walked through the doorway, Rusty said, "Pull up a kitchen chair and sit in the middle of the living room, hero."

Buck complied and sat down. Rusty undid Terry's handcuffs and instructed him to get the duct tape from the kitchen table. He told Terry to bind Buck's wrists and ankles while he kept the gun trained on Buck.

Once Buck was secured, Rusty said, "Okay, Terrance, hands behind your back." He snapped the cuffs on Terry.

"Hold on, that wasn't our deal. You said you would let Terry go," Buck shouted angrily.

"I lied, I lied, I lied." Rusty laughed as he brought another chair and motioned for Terry to sit.

"What are you trying to prove, Sykes?"

"I'm not tryin' to prove anythin' you don't already know. I told you a long time ago that I'd get even. I got a lot of scores to settle. I already settled one score and got even with my whore of a cheatin' wife. I killed her lover with her fuckin' gun. How do you like that for irony? Originally, I was gonna frame Brenda for Wayne Blackmore's murder, but that didn't quite work out. Now it's Terry's turn to die. Do you have a plan to save him, Mr. Hero? I don't think so. Hard to do when you're tied to a chair."

Stalling for time, Buck said, "You're full of shit Sykes; the Catalini brothers killed Wayne Blackmore. We've got their recorded confession.

"No, they didn't. I shot Blackmore right between the fuckin' eyes with this little ole Lady Smith & Wesson." He waved the gun in the air. "I bought this gun for Brenda for Christmas a few years ago, and I don't think she was too happy with her present. She thought a druggie had stolen it from her car a few weeks ago. I guess I'm that druggie. It turned out to be the gift that keeps giving," Rusty laughed.

"How did you know she was having an affair?" Buck asked, hoping he would keep talking.

"After she returned from a real estate seminar in Bangor last January, I figured somethin' was up. She started makin' up lame excuses about havin' to work late showin' property. At that time of year, things are still dead in the real estate market. I gave her the benefit of the doubt, but this kept goin' on for a few months. One day in early April, I followed her, and she came to your cabin. There was a black Cadillac in the driveway. I hid in the bushes and watched as a man came out and wrapped his arms around her. They kissed passionately and then went inside. That's when I knew she was cheatin' on me. I should've killed them both on the spot. That's when I came up with a plan. As I already told you, I stole her gun from the glove compartment of her car. Originally, I planned to kill her and her lover. One night, I followed Brenda to your cabin, but she didn't stay long enough for me to carry out my plan. After she left, I snuck inside and found her lover in the main bedroom. He had just finished packing a suitcase when I surprised him. He looked shocked when he saw me standin' in the doorway with a gun in my hand. He asked me who I was. I laughed and told him I was his executioner. Before he could speak, I shot him right between the fuckin' eyes. I guess all that target practice I'd been doin' paid off. I went out to my car and grabbed a pair of latex gloves. Then I packed up his clothes and personal effects and removed his watch, ring, credit cards, and all his money, leavin' no ID on his body. I found a broom and backed out of the cabin, sweepin' away my footprints on the dusty floor. I took the keys to his fancy Cadillac, tossed his suitcase into the trunk, and drove it down the boat ramp straight into the lake. I jumped out just before it went into the water. It floated for a few seconds, then it disappeared. I got into my car and left."

"I thought you said you planned to frame Brenda for Wayne Blackmore's murder?"

"I was gonna, but I couldn't figure out how to make it look believable. I decided to let Brenda live knowin' that she would feel responsible for his death. Anyway, she's goin' to jail for a while for killin' your sweet little girlfriend—enough talk. You're just tryin' to buy yourself more time and distract me from my plan. You think you're so fuckin' smart, Mr. NYPD detective."

"And what plan is that?" Buck asked.

"The plan to kill you two assholes. I already killed two scumbags, so two more won't be a problem."

"Wait a minute, Sykes. You said you killed two scumbags. One would be Wayne Blackmore. Who's the other?"

"Why don't you take a wild guess?"

"I don't have a fucking clue… unless… holy shit… your father? You killed your father?"

"Bingo, you win the prize, asshole."

"You killed your father? I don't believe it. The newspaper said he died of a heart attack."

"The newspaper was wrong. One night, when he was drunk, I helped out a little. When he passed out on his bed, I put a pillow over his face and made sure that bastard didn't wake up. He had liver cirrhosis and probably would've died in a year or two. My old man was a mean son of a bitch, a real fuckin' monster. Every time he got drunk, he would find some excuse to beat the shit out of my mom and me. He made our lives a livin' hell. As far as the world knows, he died of a heart attack. There was no autopsy, and his body was cremated the next day. There was no funeral because we couldn't afford one, and even if we could afford one, we wouldn't have wasted money on that asshole. And besides, no one would've come anyway."

After listening to Rusty's story about killing his father, Buck said,

"Killing Terry and me won't solve your problems. You need help—the kind that only a shrink can provide."

Rusty laughed. "Maybe I'm crazy, but you won't be around to find out."

"You're not crazy. You're a fucking lunatic, Sykes. You'll never get away with it."

While all this was going on, Jim had been listening to every word. I can't believe what I'm hearing. Rusty has problems, but I never thought he could murder someone. One just never knows! He must be a fucking psychopath!

Jim silently crept onto the porch, his Glock in his hand. He peered through the window and saw Rusty standing facing Buck and Terry.

He heard Rusty say, "I don't care if I get away with it. You two are responsible for ruinin' mine and Brenda's fuckin' lives."

"Think of your two children," Buck said calmly. "Who will look after them if you and Brenda are in jail?"

"They're stayin' with Brenda's mom and dad, and they'll look after them. And besides, it's none of your fuckin' business, asshole," Rusty yelled as he went over and punched Buck on the side of his mouth.

Buck could feel blood dripping from his split lower lip but showed no sign of pain. The punch had hurt, but he didn't want to give Rusty the satisfaction of seeing him wince.

After Rusty had backed up, Terry finally built up the courage to speak. "Rusty, I told you I was sorry. I don't know what else you want me to do?"

Again, Rusty laughed sadistically. "I want you to die, blabbermouth, and Buckley to watch. He can't protect you this time. Do you have any last words, Terrance? And don't say you're fuckin' sorry again. That won't save you. After he watches you die, he's next. It's time to even the score."

As Rusty raised the gun and pointed it at Terry, Jim burst through the door and fired, the bullet penetrating the back of Rusty's head. Blood and brain matter splattered in all directions. His body crumpled like a rag doll. Rusty fell forward, hitting Buck, and the chair toppled backward. Buck's head hit the floor with a resounding thud, stunning him briefly. After the stars faded, he looked up with blurry eyes. Rusty stared back at him, eyes wide open, a slight grin still on his face.

"Are you okay, B.J.?" Jim asked. He was out of breath, and his hands were shaking. It was the first time he had killed another human being.

"Yeah, I'm fine, but that was too close for comfort. Glad you talked me into letting you come along."

"How about you, Terry? Are you good?" Jim asked.

"Other than almost having a heart attack and shitting my pants, I'm okay. I thought for sure I was going to die. I must have said ten Hail Marys, and I'm not even a Catholic."

After Jim had freed Terry and Buck, he said, "Well, I'd better call this mess in and get a few people out of bed. We could be here for a while."

"I don't know about you two, but I need a drink," Buck said.

He went to the refrigerator and grabbed everyone a beer.

None of them slept that night. By the time the authorities had processed the scene, statements taken, and Rusty's body removed, it was almost noon.

Two days later, just as Rusty had said, Brenda's Lady Smith & Wesson, after testing, turned out to be the weapon used in the murder. The ballistics report confirmed that the slug found in Wayne Blackmore's head matched Brenda's gun.

Since the Catalini brothers were in jail for Wayne Blackmore's murder, Paul Prentice was informed of the new evidence, and the murder charge was dropped. However, they were still on the hook for loan sharking and extortion. Pending the findings of the Boston PD, they could still face additional charges regarding the murder of the two Boston police officers.

Three days after Rusty's death, Buck and Jim went to the Penobscot County Jail at the request of the Catalini brothers. They wanted to clarify what happened on March 30th. After the location, time, and date had been recorded, the interview began.

Jim: "Please state your full names for the record."

Joe: "Joseph Alberto Catalini"

Carmen: "Carmen Antonio Catalini"

Jim: "Would you please start at the beginning as events unfolded on the specified date."

Carmen: "My brother and I followed Wayne Blackmore from his house in Bangor to a cabin on Pushaw Lake."

Joe: "We wanted to give him a few minutes to settle in, so we parked our car off the main road just before the driveway leading to the cabin."

Buck: "Why did you follow Mr. Blackmore?"

Carmen: "He owed us money from a gambling debt, and we wanted to discuss the payment and terms of the loan."

Buck: "Did you go there to threaten Mr. Blackmore by telling him you would kill his wife and two sons if he didn't pay up?"

Joe: "We intended to scare him so he would repay the loan without delay. He kept giving us lame excuses as to why he couldn't come up with the money."

Jim: "Did you meet with Mr. Blackmore to discuss the loan repayment?"

Carmen: "No, we didn't."

Buck: "What happened to prevent that from occurring?"

Joe: "Just before we reached the road where Mr. Blackmore had turned off, a car sped past us and turned onto the same road. We parked in a secluded spot where we could watch the laneway and decided to wait."

Jim: "Then what happened?"

Carmen: "Fifteen minutes later, the car exited the driveway and drove away. Thinking the coast was clear, we were about to try again when another car drove past us and turned into the laneway. We waited, and about a half-hour later, the car appeared and sped away."

Buck: "Did you get a look at the drivers of the cars?"

Joe: "No. It was too dark. We waited a few more minutes and decided to go when the coast was clear."

Buck: "When you got to the cabin, what happened?"

Carmen: "When we arrived, Wayne Blackmore's car wasn't there. We thought that was unusual."

Jim: "Why did you think that was unusual?"

Carmen: "Because we didn't see him leave. We walked to the front of the cabin, and the door was wide open. We weren't sure what to make of that, so we cautiously went inside. There was no sound, and everything seemed normal until we entered the main bedroom. That's where we found Wayne Blackmore dead on the floor. That scared the shit out of us. We weren't going there to kill him; we only wanted to discuss the loan. It looked like someone had swept the floor, but they didn't do a good job. Not wanting to leave our footprints in the dust, we found a broom and a dustpan, and Joe swept the floor as we backed out of the cabin. He hid the broom and dustpan in the woods, and we took off. Just like the lyrics of that country song, that's our story, and we're stickin' to it." Carmen laughed.

Jim: "Okay, that does it for now. Thank you."

Jim recorded the location, date, and time the interview concluded.

Their story appeared to be mostly true. Off the record, they said that at Wayne Blackmore's funeral service, they had asked Donna Blackmore to repay her husband's loan with interest—but said nothing about threatening to kill her and her boys if she refused to pay.

A week after Rusty's death, the investigation by the Maine State Police Internal Affairs Unit concluded that it was a good shooting. Jim was off the hook. Case closed!

Brenda took Rusty's death hard at first. When she learned Rusty stole her gun, killed Wayne Blackmore, and had initially planned to frame her for his murder, her attitude changed dramatically.

The cremation of Rusty's body took place two days after his death, and there was no autopsy or funeral service.

Mark and Jennifer remained in Orono with Brenda's mother and father. The girls received grief counseling to help them deal with the traumatic events involving their parents.

On the day of Brenda's sentencing, after considering her age at the time of Doreen Warren's death, Judge Roberts sentenced her to seven years at the Maine Correctional Center for Women in Wingham, Maine. With good behavior, Brenda could be eligible for parole in three or four years.

Donna Blackmore deposited one hundred and ten thousand dollars into the account the Catalini brothers had provided—not a penny more. They would need the money to pay Carl Bono, their high-priced defense lawyer. Their trial was scheduled to take place starting the first week of November.

Since the only fingerprints on the bag of heroin were those of Wayne Blackmore, the case became a dead file. No one could figure out where the dope had come from or what he intended to do with it.

Wayne Blackmore's ring and watch turned up in a Bangor pawnshop and returned to Donna Blackmore.

Since she knew nothing about the real estate business, Donna Blackmore sold All-Star Realty, Inc. to Carl Parker. After closing the deal, she took Billy and Bobby on a two-week vacation to Disney World.

Having been told the story of their daughter's death, Doreen Warren's parents finally had closure. They expressed their heartfelt thanks to the Orono Police Department. They thanked Terry Wells for having the courage to come forward after twenty-eight years and tell the story of what had happened to their daughter on June 25, 1988. Doreen's parents sent a special thank you to Jim and Buck for solving the mystery of their daughter's death.

With the puzzle of Doreen's death resolved, Buck felt he finally had closure. His nightmares of that tragic night stopped, but he still had the odd dream about the murder of Cheryl Jenkins. Most nights, he slept soundly.

A few days after the recapture of the Catalini brothers, Brad Strongman surprised Jim with a phone call congratulating him and

Buck on their excellent work. Maybe Strongman isn't that bad after all. *Nah, he's still a jerk!*

Buck officially moved into his renovated cabin a few weeks after Rusty's death. Jim and Shawna drove out to help him set up his two beds and to arrange the rest of his new living room and kitchen furniture. The final touch was when Jim hung a large oil painting over the fireplace. Painted by a local artist, it portrayed a young Buck and his grandfather, with smiles on their faces, fishing in his grandfather's old wooden rowboat. The painting was a housewarming gift from the Barkowsky family.

Everyone grabbed a beer and retired to the living room when the work was finished.

Shawna smiled and said, "This must be a happy day for you, Buck."

"It sure is, Shawna. The cabin looks great! I love the painting of my grandfather and me. It brings back a lot of fond memories. It's almost like he's in the cabin watching over me, just like he did when I was a kid."

"Yeah," Jim said, "the artist did a terrific job. The picture looks so life-like."

"Thanks to you two, Kristina and Nicolas, it's a gift I'll cherish for the rest of my life. I'm pleased with the way everything turned out."

"Your grandfather would be so proud of what you've accomplished, Buck," Shawna said.

Suddenly, gravel crunched, and horns honked in the laneway.

"Surprise," Jim and Shawna yelled.

"What the hell's going on?" Buck said, looking confused.

"It's a little housewarming party," Jim said.

Car doors slammed, and a few seconds later, smiling faces appeared in the doorway. Buck was speechless when Chief Durham and his wife Kathy, Captain Tony Timpano and his wife Elaine, Elsie Brody and her husband John, Colin Kelly and his wife Susan, Mayor Steve Smith and his wife Mary, retired Chief Barker, Kristina, Nicolas, and Terry Wells crowed into the living room. Everyone had brought food and housewarming gifts.

Colin Kelly had rounded up the members of his old band, the Shamrocks, and foot-stomping Irish music filled the air a half hour later.

The next afternoon, anchored over a deep fishing hole, slightly hungover, Buck and Jim were relaxing, enjoying the warm sunshine in Buck's grandfather's old boat that he had completely restored.

"Well," Buck said, "this is the life," sipping on his beer. "That was quite the surprise yesterday. What a great party! It was good to hear the Shamrocks play again."

"Yeah, it was fun. The band hasn't missed a beat. It's nice to take a day off and relax. I wonder what the rich people are doing today?" Jim laughed.

"If I had to guess, I'd say they're probably at home counting their money," Buck chuckled.

"Speaking of money, Shawna and I don't have much money to count, but we count our blessings daily. I have a great job, and Shawna enjoys owning the salon. We have a nice home, two super kids, and a good friend in you, Buck."

"Ah, you're making me blush," Buck grinned. "The feeling is mutual, my friend. I couldn't ask for better friends than you and Shawna."

"The other night, while you talked with Rusty, I was shocked when he confessed to killing Wayne Blackmore. I couldn't believe what I had heard. All the evidence pointed to the Catilini brothers, but neither of their guns matched the slug that killed Blackmore. Why did the brothers tell Donna Blackmore they would take care of her and her boys like they took care of her husband?"

"They were bluffing, Telly. They pretended they killed Wayne Blackmore to scare Donna to get her money. They wouldn't have said they killed her husband if they suspected the conversation was being recorded."

"The brothers are off the hook for Blackmore's murder, but they still have to answer for loan sharking and extortion. Even though they didn't pull the trigger when the Boston police officers were gunned down, the brothers could still face further charges once the investigation concludes," Jim said.

"Once convicted on loan sharking and extortion charges, the brothers will be in prison for a long time," Buck said.

"Something's been bothering me, Buck."

"What is it, Telly?"

"I never killed anyone before. The night I shot, Rusty keeps flashing through my head. I've even had nightmares about it. I know, as a Marine, you had to kill the enemy in the Gulf War, and you had to shoot your partner's killer and probably more bad guys in your job. How do you deal with it?"

"That's a hard question to answer, Telly. Everybody deals with that kind of stress in different ways. Some people can forget about it, erase it from their minds, and not let it bother them, while others have difficulty dealing with it. As for me, I already told you the story of my problems with PTSD after returning from the Gulf War. Cheryl's killing took me on a guilt trip because I thought I could have saved her if I had done something differently. Now I realize there's probably nothing I could have done to change the outcome. If you let it, it will eat away at you, and it can destroy you. In my case, I'm trying to put it behind me and get on with my life. Getting away from New York City has helped immensely. My advice is to keep busy, so you don't have time to consider it. I've found time is the best healer. You might want to see a shrink if you still have problems dealing with it. It helped me. It could help you as well."

"Thanks for the advice, partner."

"You're welcome, Telly."

"By the way, Buck, are you returning to the NYPD, or will you retire? Just think, if you retire, you could spend every summer on the lake enjoying life and go to Florida in the winter to escape the cold. Maybe I could even talk Chief Durham into hiring you as a part-time consultant. You could work with me on all the homicides we have to deal with," Jim laughed. "Like one or two every five years or so."

Buck laughed too. "If I had to rely on working on all the local homicides, I'd starve to death. Anyway, I haven't made a decision yet. It'll probably come down to the money, but living here on the lake won't take much. If they offer me a decent retirement package, I might consider it. I could get used to summers here at the cabin, that's for sure, and spending the winter months in Florida sounds like a great idea. What more could a guy want?"

Jim grinned. "To catch a few fish. That's what I want!"

"Yeah, that would be nice."

Buck glanced at the cabin. He could swear his grandpa was sitting on the front porch, drinking a beer, staring at Buck and Jim in his old rowboat. His grandfather smiled and waved.

As Buck smiled and waved back, he felt a sharp tug on his line!

www.ingramcontent.com/pod-product-compliance
Lightning Source LLC
Chambersburg PA
CBHW050934120626
46552CB00001B/194